SURFER JOE

Robert Curtis

Martin Sisters Publishing

Published by

Ivy House Books, a division of Martin Sisters Publishing, LLC

www.martinsisterspublishing.com

Copyright © 2012 by Robert Curtis

ISBN: 978-1-937273-28-6

Literary Fiction

Editor: Elizabeth Newton

Back Cover Photo Courtesy of Rob Willing

Printed in the United States of America
Martin Sisters Publishing, LLC

DEDICATION

The Surfaris, the Beach Boys, Jan and Dean, and all the other surf bands that surfers hated; and to the wave riders, every last one.

An imprint of Martin Sisters Publishing, LLC

PROLOGUE

The mighty breath of the wind blows down along the face of the sea. It lifts and drops with the rising and falling thunder of the waves. The sunlight and the pressing air from above quicken that breath, and the waves, rolling wild and sonorous, grow dangerous, rising to the size of small mountains.

Out there, a lonely figure, paddling out on a fragile board of foam and fiberglass resin, works his way up the face of an incoming wave.

It's bright sunlight, a sky of mystic blue, and the waves, maybe ten, maybe thirty feet high, break cleanly over the top, rolling and running left out into a sculpting tube of effervescent green, vivacious blue, then bright, white, air-choked water as the tube explodes. In its perfect state, it grows into a pipeline straight into the heart of the sea.

The surf rider ducks into the crest slicing his way to the other side and emerges from the back like a mountain climber rising over the summit. He drops down the back side into a trough of momentary calm with another wave farther out in the set, birthing into a swell, another rise.

The surf rider turns his board and waits, watching over his shoulder, vigilant for that mounting change in the water, and he feels it underneath. He lay down quickly on the board and begins to paddle in long, smooth strokes to chase the wave, and he catches it cleanly. He jumps to his knees and rises in one graceful move.

Suddenly, it's as if the horizon, that far-off gentle curve at the end of the earth looms like a monster you didn't know was there. It rises under and just behind the surf rider on his flashy but frail board. What kind of spiritual power is this? The rider is but a pinch of sand and sea, and the aqueous leviathan, incalculable tons of wave, curls and storms toward that momentary apocalypse when it breaks and rolls like the end of the world. It's giant, white lip closes down, charges, and explodes with a frenzy that's run amok.

And through the birthing and charge off the lip, the surf rider crouches to let the wall of water roll over top forming that perfect, aqueous tube—that pipeline. As he runs, the surf rider stretches out a hand to slice through the inside face, carving destiny and the inescapable songs of raw creation. He peers out the window of the green room, Emerald City in the Land of Oz.

And when it finally hits—a thunderous green or broiling blue armada—the rider lets loose, turns away to be chased by the air-choked spray, peeling like the last moments of a comet hurtling across the starry sky.

And he flies.

Chapter One

My older brother Joe Connors was the best of the best. He emerged out of the Pacific Palisades after graduating from Saint Monica Catholic High School in 1965 to become the greatest surfer that was ever seen. At least in my eyes he was the greatest. His best friend, Rod Wilson, could have become the best too, but he didn't have the same passion Joe did. Both loved to surf and they loved the surfing scene—the cars, the girls, the sun, and the waves, but Joe was obsessed. And his obsession was apparent.

At first Joe wouldn't take me with him when he went out to practice. Practice to Joe meant he would drive himself to what I would later find out was a Zen level of surfing. He smiled and told me that I was too young at sixteen, a gremmie. I told him that he was out of his mind. He'd begun surfing at thirteen years old, and I started at about twelve it didn't seem fair that he'd leave me at home when I was almost seventeen. I didn't have my driver's license yet so I was stuck. But once Rod began to get other ideas in December of 1966, I went with Joe all the time. I figured he wanted me to be there so that someone could tell Mom if the worst happened. Even great surfers were not immune to the fickleness of ten to fifteen foot waves; untold tons of water, rolling and crashing without the slightest regard for any kind of life. The ocean was a great equalizer.

Surfing seemed a kind of sanctuary for Joe, the free-life, water, sun, and sand. By 1967 the world was coming apart. There was a war in Southeast Asia, riots at colleges all across the country, race problems (even though a civil rights bill had been signed four years earlier), and people appeared to come unglued everywhere. There were also the hippies, free love people that I didn't mind in the slightest, hoping as a hormonal sixteen year old boy would for some "free love". There wasn't much romantic love at home after my father left us for some secretary he met at work. He moved to Texas leaving us stranded with a mother who knew nothing about becoming a man. We never doubted that she loved us. But not having a role model made it tough. Joe and I relied on the likes of Rod's father, Dave, an ex-Marine who fought in Korea, distinguishing himself and earning a Bronze Star for heroism. He seemed like a hero to me, six foot four inches tall with a short-cropped hair cut and a booming Drill Instructor voice that he developed over the ten years after Korea when he stayed in the Corps to help mold more Marines. Only the accident kept him out of the service—a tank rolled over his leg and crushed it. His leg had so many steel pins in it that he had to stay away from large magnets. He walked with a limp and a cane but he still looked imposing. Rod's mother had passed away just after he graduated from high school, so all five of us together were kind of like a family.

In January of 1967, the war in Southeast Asia was escalating and Dave Wilson was outraged that he couldn't be there to protect other Marines. He became evermore frustrated as the television networks kept showing a nightly scoreboard that we didn't yet know was a lie—Us: 5 dead, Them: 1005—along with photographs and film at eight. We saw a constant stream of images of dead and dying American servicemen in places like the Mekong

Delta, the Iron Triangle, and the Ashau Valley. There were plenty of photographs and films about napalm.

I knew about napalm and it made me shiver just to think about it.

In late February of 1967 Rod began to talk about joining the Marines. Dozens of his and Joe's classmates from high school had already joined the service or had been drafted. Why Rod and my brother hadn't yet gone was beyond me, though I suspected why Joe wasn't interested.

"Come on, Joe," Rod said as he applied a second coat of wax to his favorite big board, a big stick or gun as surfers called it. "Man, everyone has gone over there to kick some Commie ass except us."

Joe was unusually calm about such things.

"And how many have come back in aluminum boxes?" Joe replied, "John Simons, and Mike Phillips, there's Pete Russell, remember him?"

Rod looked exasperated.

"I know, war's hell, but are you afraid?" he replied, almost challengingly.

Joe half smiled at this. Coming down a laid-out barrel off a thirty foot wave was not child's play by the stretch of anyone's imagination. That much water could crush you like a gnat in a less than a heartbeat; same as a bullet from a Commie.

"What do you think?" Joe replied, looking Rod in the eye, "Am I afraid?"

Rod broke eye contact and went back to his wax.

"It'll be over before we know it and then what will we tell our grandkids?"

Joe smiled again, that wry smile of his that told the rest of us that he knew something we couldn't even comprehend if we tried.

"I'll tell them that I didn't get killed in the war and that's the reason they're alive!" Joe said without the slightest hint of sarcasm or rancor. It was true; if he didn't go, he didn't get shot or blown up by some kid with a bomb in his straw hat.

"Funny." Rod replied sarcastically as he shook his head, "I'm joining up before I get drafted. I don't want to get put in the Army. My father would never forgive me."

Joe shrugged and that was that.

Rod had not done anything for the almost two years since they graduated. He just surfed and drove the old Woody around—a 1934 Ford station wagon with wood panels on the doors—that he and Joe owned mutually. My brother worked at a surf shop just south of Malibu and had earned enough money to take six classes at the community college. The classes were in oceanography and physics. But Joe's dream was to continue being a surfer the rest of his days and open a string of shops from Peru to Hawaii. Yet there was something about science; about the way the world turned that seemed to intrigue him.

Joe talked about science every now and again, saying things none of us could understand. He told us that the universe was connected at the tiniest level, smaller than atoms, bundles of light that were sometimes particles, sometimes both. His grades in high school were actually well above average. He got into college part time without any problem. The college advisors told him that he could get into one of the state's universities with a scholarship, even Cal Poly, impressed as they were with his understanding of physics. He would sometimes tell us about waves in the ocean, draw strange mathematical formulas in the sand with a stick. "Hyperbolic tangents," he'd begin, "that moment when the surface tension is broken by the energy. The Tube…" He'd drift off for a few moments and then continue, "Gnarly swells that go abruptly from deep to shallow water, reefs. Perfect rolls, the Emerald Room."

Joe spent a significant amount of time working on some kind of paper. He called it his "everything" paper. When I asked him what he meant he told me, "It's the E8; some dude found it in 1887 and all the other dudes have been working on it ever since." He told me that everything is connected and that he wanted to prove it. When I looked at the paper it was a mess of mathematical symbols, almost like he was writing a story, not in words, but in symbols. It was a little eerie for me.

The college advisors also suggested Joe enlist in the service because the government gave money to people to go to college after they completed their tours of duty. It was called the GI Bill, something our own father had used to get a business degree and a decent job in a corporation. But it didn't keep him from running off to Texas and divorcing our mother.

"What's the E8 again?" I asked for the millionth time.

My girlfriend, Laci, always seemed to have a little understanding about Joe's theory; she took physics and had a mind that could think of more than two things at a time, unlike me. I thought of surfing and her, or her and surfing every other day. At sixteen, just a few months younger than I was, she was a dream. Short and petite, she wore her blonde hair short, pixie-style. Her bright blue eyes sparkled and she was one of the smartest and most popular girls in school. For some reason, however, she liked me although I was nobody.

Joe talked about elementary particles, the electromagnetic force, the strong force, the weak force, and gravity. There were quarks and all manner of things happening out in space any of which could mess up our day on Earth.

Joe said he wanted to track neutrinos, little zappers that flew through everything except, for some mathematical reason, a surfer coming off a wave of thirty feet or more. When I asked why Joe would say it was a mystery. I asked more questions than I knew I'd ever understand the answers to.

"Like the Host in Church that Father McNamara tried to get me to understand turned into the body of Jesus?" I struggled to find a comparison with something familiar.

"Yeah," Joe replied, "Or like a barrel that suddenly drops out. Nobody should be able to ride a wave higher than thirty feet— angles, force, motion, time, the Second Law of Thermodynamics."

"Thermo what?" I sputtered, already feeling the pressure in my head.

"It's Newton's Second Law of Thermodynamics, the Conservation of Energy," Laci interjected like a special-ed teacher trying to explain the wind to a learning-challenged student.

I scratched my head and looked at the two of them.

"And why do these neutrino things not shoot through surfers on thirty-foot waves?" I plied, hoping for the kindergarten version.

"Because a surfer riding at thirty feet or higher is at the edge of the universe, outside of time, limited to a two-by-six or two-by-ten foot space. That's why Hawaiians are so happy."

I stared at Joe, my eyes asking what my mind could not.

"They ride fifteen foot boards," he'd reply with a smile, "They have more space."

It sounded definitive.

Joe would write things on napkins and paper bags, occasionally even on his surf board. He did it using crayons, especially when his board was losing wax.

Naturally I couldn't keep up with him; I was the ordinary son. Whenever he could Joe would sit on his board and talk to dolphins. He'd sit and listen to their chatter, ask questions, and take notes.

"The dolphins know a lot about the E8," Joe said, "They have some interesting ideas."

I looked at Laci.

"They have interesting ideas he says," I repeated motioning toward Joe, "Dolphins."

Laci would smile, pat me on the arm, and then go into her special-ed teacher mode, "Cetaceans are among the most intelligent creatures on the planet. Some say they are even more intelligent than humans because they had enough sense to stay in the oceans."

I looked at Laci and then at Joe.

"You two are conspiring together," I said with a knowing smile.

They both looked innocent enough.

"What is the E8 again?" I asked.

"It's a pattern, dude," Joe replied patiently. "All fields of the standard model and gravity are unified as an E8 principal bundle connection. A non-compact real form of the E8 Lie algebra has G2 and F4 sub-algebras which break down to strong su(3), electroweak su(2) x u(1), gravitational so(3,1), the frame-Higgs, and three generations of fermions related by triality."

I stared blankly at Joe and then turned toward Laci.

"He made that up," I said flatly.

She shrugged and a small smile touched the corners of her mouth.

Joe was a big fan of Albert Einstein, someone he considered one of the smartest men ever. He often told me that Einstein was a patent clerk when he came up with the special theory of relativity, $E=MC^2$, which everyone knew as "Energy equals Mass times the Velocity of Light squared."

I didn't know what it amounted to. In fact, I barely knew what two trains leaving from cities at opposite ends of the country, traveling at sixty miles an hour with some kid named Doug on one and another kid named Pam on the other train, meant.

There were days when Joe would sit on the beach in Malibu up near the surf shop, and think. Occasionally, he would take out a ratty notebook and scribble equations in it. If I was with him, I took out my notebook and scribbled words in it, more poems to inspire Laci to stick around. When Laci was with us, I'd sit right next to her, touching, and it was almost like lovemaking. I could feel the heat coming off her skin and it made my heart beat a little faster.

One day Rod broached the subject of enlisting again. "I really wish you would reconsider signing up," Rod pressed. "It would mean a lot to me knowing you'd have my back. The two of us could hit those Viet Cong hard."

"I think I'll keep hitting the waves," Joe replied with a grin, "What do you think little brother?"

I stared at Joe for a moment and then glanced at Rod. What did I know? I was just a kid and this was the first time Joe ever asked my opinion on something so important.

"I dunno," I mumbled, "I think you ought to keep surfing."

Joe grinned again.

"See, Pat thinks I should keep surfing," he said as he held out his hand for me to give him five. I slapped his hand triumphantly.

"What does he know?" Rod replied with a shake of his head, "He's just a kid!"

I scowled slightly but didn't say anything because, after all, he was right

"We're all born to do different things," Joe said, "Some are doctors, some ministers, some mechanics, and some soldiers. Mine is to surf."

"Serving your country for a couple of years doesn't mean you have to be a soldier forever," Rod replied, "You could go right back to surfing."

Joe returned Rod's stare.

"Come on," Rod repeated his earlier plea. "We can go together, look out for each another."

Joe shrugged.

"It's just not my thing," he replied, "And I don't see how it could be your thing either."

Rod shook his head and returned to waxing his board.

"I already signed up," he nearly whispered.

Joe stopped waxing his board to ponder this monumental decision. It was a life changer for certain.

"I leave for San Diego a week after Spring Break," he added quietly.

Joe looked up at Rod and then smiled.

"Then we better get as much surfing in as possible," he said, "What do you think, little brother?"

I nodded enthusiastically. The more practice I could get, the better I'd be; and I wanted to be like Joe.

Laci came strolling out onto the sand from the parking lot.

She seemed to enjoy watching me surf and yet she would hold her breath as long as I did when I wiped-out at the top of a curl. She also liked my adolescent poetry, which I suddenly started writing after I met her one day at school out near the cafeteria. She was dropped off early each day by her father on his way to work and it didn't take me long to fall for her. It was almost incomprehensible to anyone who knew us., Laci was a varsity cheerleader and was picked to be part of the royalty at every prom and dance the school had. And Pat Connors? People barely knew my name. Still, I started writing poetry, if it could be called that. But I managed pubescent metaphors clear enough for Laci to know they were about her. She treated my poems like they were holy writs or something, reading them carefully, smiling, and developing a tear now and again. I guess nobody ever took the time to write anything for her although I could not understand why.

One thing was for certain, Laci's very presence in my life made me want to work harder in school. My grades started to show it and soon I was on the principal's honor roll. Nobody knew it, however, except me and the principal.

I had just dropped down off the curl on a four-foot wave and was carving the face when I spotted her. I promptly fell off my board and was spit out by the white water. Abashedly, I gathered up my board and headed for the shore.

"Hey there," I said as she stopped in front me and raised her sun glasses to squint at me in the bright sun.

"Hey yourself," she replied with a kind of oafish grin. "How are you doing out here today?"

I glanced back out at the ocean. The off-shore breeze was moderate, which meant that the waves were moderate, no higher than four-foot. Certainly not point surf, but they were enough to make me respect them. Falling once before, I was hammered and nearly knocked into an undertow but I kicked hard and managed to make it back to the surface. It was a trick Joe taught me; don't wait for the undertow to grab you because its job was to kill you outright, he said.

We'd lost a kid about my age the summer before; he went up on the curl, over the top, lost his footing and disappeared under a nasty fifteen footer that swept him under and out to sea. They found him three miles down two days later. Apparently, he'd also had a run in with a shark or a dolphin with an attitude while out there floating aimlessly at the mercy of the currents. Joe led those of us who regularly used Malibu Beach in a kind of memorial service. He called it a surfer's service where we'd light small candles like those you see in a church, place them on a surf board and then walk solemnly back to our cars. It was moving.

Joe gave the candles to the kid's parents and told them we'd held a surfer's service out on the beach. They both cried and were grateful.

"Doing okay," I replied, "They're not running very high today, not much breeze."

Laci always liked to hear that because that meant I wasn't risking my life like a fool. For some reason, she liked my face.

"You know," she said, "You ought to write some poems about surfing instead of just about me all the time."

I smiled at the suggestion.

"But you're my muse," I replied wanting to kiss her madly right there on the beach, "Whatever that is."

She laughed.

"I'm glad I'm your muse," she said, "So write me some poems about surfing!"

I stared at her long enough to know she was serious. Maybe my stupid poems were finally boring her. Maybe I'd try writing something about surfing, maybe something about my brother, Joe. He was a good subject.

"All right," I replied, "I'll write something about surfing, let the board be my muse."

She reached and took my hand and pouted ever so slightly.

My hormones went into overdrive and I was quick with my board to hide my embarrassment.

"But I'm your muse," she said sultrily.

I laughed to cover my sudden nervousness.

"Yeah, you're a good muse."

Suddenly, she reached up and brushed my lips with hers. I was so thunderstruck that I couldn't make a move and was certain that my heart had stopped.

Had I been older and more experienced, I would have known the sign and would have reciprocated in the best possible manner. It would have made people on the beach pause and stop what they were doing. It would have made surfers fall off their boards.

"What was that for?" I asked, my voice shaky with the after effects of three or four gallons of adrenaline suddenly pumped into my system.

"For inspiration," she replied with a smile as she swung around and headed back for her car. I watched as if it was the last thing on earth I would ever do.

Poetry in motion.

That night, at home in my bedroom, I took out a piece of paper and began to write;

Big waves up from the sea,
My board is stallion for me,

I looked at it and read silently out loud. I didn't know much about meter but it sounded ok. I continued writing:

With sun and surf I boldly go,
To reach the curl its top I throw;

That was pretty cool, I thought, maybe even inspired.

Early the next morning on Saturday, Joe and I jumped into the Woody to pick up Rod and head for the beach. When we arrived Rod was packing.

"I thought you said you weren't leaving until the week after Spring Break?" Joe asked.

"Never hurts to get ready ahead of time," Rod replied. "The bus for San Diego will pull up and I'll be gone. It will be at night. They want to make sure we arrive in the dark so they can scare us."

I wondered what he meant.

"Okay," Joe said, "So you leave the week after Spring Break. How about coming with us this morning?"

Rod stopped for a moment and looked around the room.

"I should visit with my family; my Dad and my cousins" he mused. "We'll have time to surf. Who knows when I'll get to see them all again after boot camp?"

It sounded foreboding but Joe just smiled and nodded.

"Why do they call it 'boot camp'?" I asked, still perplexed about the whole military thing.

"Because the lowest thing on a Marine is his boots," Rod replied with a grin, "The new recruit is the lowest thing in the Marine Corps...a boot!"

Suddenly, it made sense...a boot! I had to laugh.

"Okay," Joe said, "We'll call you later about some surfing."

I nodded solemnly because it seemed like a solemn duty. Rod agreed and for some reason, we each shook his hand. It seemed like the right thing to do, part of a kind of rite of passage to manhood. We always shook the hands of adults we met and we could tell that Rod was right at the edge.

With that, Joe and I piled into the Woody and headed for the beach just south of Malibu. The beach was near the surf shop where Joe worked. He had three of his trophies there and seven others at home. People would come into the store and stare at the trophies with both admiration and envy. Sometimes I thought the owner had Joe work there just for show; the shop with the best surfer around, that sort of thing. Joe thought the same thing sometimes, but he didn't care. When he wasn't surfing, he could talk surfing and trade stories with the other surfers. It was the perfect job for Joe.

Once we arrived at the beach, everyone there began to congregate around us. One kid, who looked a little younger than I was, wanted my autograph—the great Joe Connors' little brother. I was a squire to the knight.

After a few minutes of pleasantries and talk, Joe would announce that he was going to hit the waves. He would take his board and dash into the water with me right behind him.

It was poetry to watch my brother surf. He'd paddle out with big long strokes, cresting the incoming waves with ease while I struggled every time. His strong body covered by the short black wetsuit, he always wore, seemed made for the water. When he passed the breaking surf just off shore, he'd wait in the calm, and behind him, the water would swell, looking like the ocean about to give birth; and in a way it was. Each time a whole, new, completely unique wave was born. Each one was a wave that would either thrill or kill depending upon which way the wind was blowing and the skill of the surfer.

Joe would wait and then lay down flat on his board until it became part of him. Then, as the wave lifted him, he'd pop up like a dancer arising to a sudden crescendo, a natural-footed surfer, his arms would extend and then he would bend his knees, sculpting his body to the movement of the water as it broke over the curl and started him downward at breakneck speed. He'd ride the wave, and if it was small, he'd carve up and across, using his momentum to stretch the run. If the wave was large, he'd drop down into the barrel and ride inside or almost inside, with tons of frantic water breaking over and over in a roar. There was nothing more beautiful than Joe in a wide-open tube, except maybe Laci.

For myself, I'd try to follow his lead down at the other end of the wave. Many times I'd wind up falling off my board, especially when I tried to turn and carve. I learned to time the fall, taking a last big breath just as I hit the water, or just as the water hit me. If I was off, then a million tons of water would knock what little breath I had out of me; then I had to fight the panic and kick myself to the surface.

Today Joe seemed to be surfing for Rod, trying to surf to perfection as a kind of monument to his friend. The crowd of onlookers would cheer, especially when Joe finally broke out over a sizeable wave, carved, and then shoved it, shooting up over the top again, spinning a three-sixty and dropping back down until he finally rode down to the shore standing up. The kids especially loved it because my brother was their hero; everybody's hero just south of Malibu out on the California coast.

Surfing was a sanctuary for me as well as for Joe. I'd forget about the troubles in the world that were making themselves known in the constant stream of stories of brothers, fathers, cousins, friends, friends of friends, who were here one day and lying inside a flag-draped coffin the next. I really didn't want my brother to go but it seemed like everyone was joining, getting called up, or burning flags on college campuses. Joe was meant to surf and he needed to do that.

I was lying on the warming sand with my board stuck upright just behind me and my eyes closed. Joe was out catching another wave, and then another. Suddenly, someone dropped down next to me on the sand and I opened my eyes to look. Before I focused, I felt a silky, warm set of lips touch mine, a little more commanding than yesterday,

It was Laci. She smiled and brushed the sand off her hands.

"Hey there," she said like she always did.

"Hey yourself," I replied as part of our greeting game.

"Have you already been out?" she asked, looking out to see Joe scoring a rare monster.

I nodded.

"Good," she said, "I wasn't here to worry about it. You can get yourself killed on your own time."

I looked up at her. This girl was going to be trouble I could somehow tell.

"I have something for you," I said as I dug into the inside pocket of my beachcombers. I stopped for a moment when I realized Laci was watching me intently. She met my eyes, blushed and turned away.

I brought out a soggy piece of paper barely readable in my penciled scrawl. I held it out and she took it reverently.

She read:

"Big wave up from the sea,
My stick is stallion to me,
With sun and surf I boldly go,
To reach the curl its top I know;
The downhill ride at break-neck
speed,
Fulfills my soul, fulfills my need."

She gazed at it for a long moment and then looked at me.

"That's really good," she said, "Really good."

I smiled. Somehow the words of my writing, adolescent as they were, were something altogether new for Laci. She loved the arts and had a beautiful singing voice. Poetry was the literature that she craved. The odd thing was I didn't know anyone else who wrote poetry, even in the school paper. I wondered what life would be like as a surfing poet, traveling around the world—Hawaii, Peru, Australia, the Solomons, bleached blonde hair, my surfboard and my surfer girl with me.

ROBERT CURTIS

Chapter Two

The surf shop where Joe worked was called Hobie's and was owned by Hobie Alder. Hobie was an older surfer who served in the Navy during World War II and then simply stayed on in Malibu after he was discharged. He learned to surf in Hawaii where the local Bras took him under their wing while the mine-sweeper he served aboard put into Oahu for repairs. In Malibu, at first, he earned a marginal living from odd jobs—compliments of general naval training—and he spent all his free time surfing. Hobie was good and had several trophies up on the shelf alongside Joe's to prove it. Later, he opened the surf shop on little more than a dream of making the perfect board in order to search for the perfect wave.

There in the surf shop Hobie and company took long, eight and ten foot foam blanks and cut them, shaped them with hand planes and sanded them to smooth perfection. Whole fiberglass cloth was laid over the foam and then resin was brushed on, allowed to hardened, and then the board was sanded and another layer was added. No two were alike and Hobie had employed an artist named Knob to make sure of that. Knob worked to bring the boards to color and life between glassing coats. I learned that Knob was called Knob because he contracted a rare tropical disease on a trip to Indonesia. As a result he lost all his hair. He had no eyebrows, no hair on his head, or even on his arms or legs. He assured me more than once that the rest of his body was as hairless as his head. Knob was from Taos, New Mexico and his inclination in art was definitely southwestern. He used ancient pueblo symbols and the whole scope of pueblo mythology to cover the boards. He viewed the typical late-60s psychedelic artwork used on most surf boards with disdain. As a result Knob's boards were the most distinctive on the coast. The only board I owned in my youth, was a repaired board that Joe recovered in two pieces from Malibu. Hobie, as a favor to Joe, stripped it down, worked it into a slightly smaller six foot, eight inch board. Then Knob painted Spider Woman emerging from First Mesa into the world onto it. When Joe brought it home to me I thought it was so cool that I didn't care that some fool fell off of it and let it smash into two pieces on the rocks. People might laugh at the small size of the board because the short board was just then coming to life in Hawaii and had yet to reach the mainland. Everyone used seven foot plus sticks in those days. Laci was amazed by the board and even Joe thought it was gnarly, and a pretty good bargain, considering it was free. I even named the board, "Spider Woman," and she helped me improve my surfing; that is, Spider Woman, and my big brother Joe.

One day in late February, Joe came home and told me that Hobie was forming a surf team that would have both seniors and juniors on it. Hobie once saw me out surfing, liked what he saw, and so he invited me to join the team. I thought Joe was kidding, playing a joke on me. But he wasn't. Hobie had surf shirts with the Hobie logo screen-printed on them and Joe gave me one. He said that the team would compete in invitationals and other contests up and down the coast of California, even at a special meet in Hawaii called Makaha on the island of Oahu.

But first we would compete locally. The Jacobs' Invitational was held in Newport Beach and it was only in its fourth year. Jacobs' kids had dominated, except when Joe surfed the contest. Hobie wanted to make things right.

The contest was held just off the Pier where the waves were kicking about three to four feet; not much for hot-dogging, but they were solid waves. When Joe, Rod, and I arrived at the beach we were greeted by a mixture of admiration for Joe and some laughs at my short board; until they saw Spider Woman painted on top. 'Awesome' was the word I heard repeated, though there was still curiosity about the short board. We signed up with Hobie and soon our whole team was there.

It was time to rock.

Jacobs' team had dominated, except for Joe of course, for the last two years. I had heard that the Jacobs' kids were snotty, big-headed, and thought they owned the waves. They were the ones who laughed but shrugged and kept quiet after everyone else gathered to admire Spider Woman.

"Artwork don't ride waves, Dude" one of the Jacobs' geniuses said. But Joe just smiled at him even though I was ready to start a riot.

"But riding waves is artwork," Joe said as he gave the kid the hang-ten sign.

The kid was momentarily confused but then half-smiled and returned the sign.

In the first heat of my first meet I was nervous. Joe told me that the only important thing about these contests was that you got to ride waves, you got to climb up and sail down, wing on the wind and wave. Trophies weren't important, accolades didn't mean that much except that you got to surf. I tried to think that way when I went out into the lineup. Kids in front of me took off, some flew and some crashed. There wasn't much razzle-dazzle, not many hot-dogs showing their stuff. When my name was called from the beach, I waited and let the first one go. The second one in the set started to rise and I thought about it but the third one looked really good. Some kid behind me in the lineup started to harass me, growing impatient for his turn. I began paddling as the sea swelled beneath me and I caught the wave right across the top and dropped down the other side. My shorty was gliding, 'in the glide' as Joe called it, and suddenly I turned up and flew back across the top of the wave, bending to take hold of my board in mid-air. As I turned back, I landed on the face a little too steep, rode for a moment and then pearled. Ten feet to the bottom and I was glad that my red face had time to cool off as I headed for the surface. When I broke water I could hear wild applause coming from the beach and I turned to see who was flying to delight the crowd. There wasn't anyone behind me coming down, and as I gathered my board I realized that the cheering was for my attempted aerial; the aerial I almost made.

No one else tried that maneuver but it just seemed natural with the shortboard which was lighter, faster, better to fly with as its cutbacks were downright gnarly. The longboards couldn't do that so I knew I had an edge even though I wiped out on my first run.

Joe was clapping as I dragged my board up onto the beach. His smile was huge and he clapped me on my back.

"Straight up, Bro!" he said enthusiastically. Everyone could see he was proud of his little brother for trying something new on his first time out in a contest.

Joe was awesome and he crushed the competition, finishing first.

When I went back out for the second heat, a kid with a Jacobs' shirt on paddled over to me.

"Dude, that was gnarly," he said with a grin, "When I saw your board at sign-up I thought 'what's this guy going to do with that dinky thing?' Now I know man, fly for real!"

I was stunned for a moment. Then he introduced himself. He was Herbie Torres and he said he'd been surfing Newport Beach since he was out of diapers.

I asked him if he was going to Makaha and he nodded with a big grin, "To the Islands, Dude!"

I smiled and took off on my second run. When I caught it, I could feel it lifting, breaking to the left which would put me closer to the Pier. I jumped up, cut left and then back up the face for a one-eighty. I straightened down, gathered some speed and then tried it again: cutback, race up and over the edge. I grabbed my board with my hand and turned it back landing at a slight angle breaking left again toward the Pier. As the wave dropped out I realized that I was still standing and the crowd noise was as loud as the waves. Instinctively I raised my hands above my head. Not even Joe had done something like that.

I made it into the semis, wiped out again, this time trying a three-sixty aerial like a dim-wit lacking cognitive gifts. When the meet was over, the trophy was Joe's. I came in fifth which was not too bad for my first try.

Hobie was ecstatic! He told me that he would make me a longboard so that I could enter the upcoming noseriding contests. He also said that he was going to make shortboards for some of the other surfers like Joe and Rod.

He didn't mind in the slightest that I came in fifth; he just saw aerials. For the first time Hobie had dreams of domination on his mind.

The following week there was a noseriding contest up off California Street in Ventura. I practiced about thirty minutes one day with Joe's longboard and almost got the hang of it. It wasn't enough to enter any competition but it was a start. When Joe, Rod, and I showed up at California Street Hobie was there with a Knob special longboard which he handed to me. On it Knob had painted a panorama of Navajo mythology with Monument Valley, the place where the great John Wayne made some of his western movies. Knob had created majestic mesas, the sun, the sky, eagles, the Navajo people and something called a Kachina on it. The Kachina was a kind of monster with a mask over the head of a dancer. Several of the other surfers gathered and looked it over. It was like being in an art gallery. The Jacobs boys kept quiet, except for Herbie Torres. Herbie freaked out when he saw the board.

"Man, that's like a piece of art, man!" he said, almost reverently. "Put it in the art gallery of the sea!"

He grinned and I thought, 'the art gallery of the sea, Herbie must be a poet or something.' That's probably why I liked him even though he was on the Jacobs' team.

My first heat was amazing. I caught the wave on top with the longboard hanging way out. Standing back like I always did, I stepped forward and tipped the board over the falls fully expecting to go down with the ship. Instead, the board shifted, hit at an angle and I crouched into a slight turn. Here was where I would normally carve up but this was a nose-riding contest. I took a deep breath and started forward, inching my way toward the nose. Suddenly, I had one foot on, my toes actually hanging over the edge. All I had to do was put the other foot forward and it was Round Two for me. And I did, that is, until I pearled. That big board came over the top and I brought my hands up to cover my head.

WHAM!

I was about ten foot under before I realized I was still alive and not broken in half. I pushed off from the bottom and could see my board. When I broke the surface I had hold of the board and rode it the rest of the way in. My scores came up and I thought someone had made an error.

Joe grinned. "Not bad, Bro," he said as he clapped me on the back, "All that practicing with my board paid off."

They weren't top scores but they were enough to put me into the second heat. I guess I did manage to hang all ten before pearling and coming up with the board. Herbie Torres did much better but then he rode a longboard all of the time. Walking the thing was no big deal to him.

My second heat was worse and I wound up in twelfth place out of twelve. Hobie was happy because his team did take the meet despite me. Hobie assured me that no one ever hangs all ten on the first try. I was something special.

The trophy? It was Joe's again, with some guy from Jacobs taking second. Rod finished third but he was already thinking about other things in his life so it didn't matter that much to him. When it came time to think about Makaha over Spring Break, Hobie said he would pay for most of the trip and we would have to raise the rest. Mom said she could pay a little. Joe told me not to worry about it at all because he had some money and he worked for Hobie.

I was not one to let anyone totally carry my burden. I broke out the old hand-push mower and began a charity urban renewal campaign with me as the charity. I went up and down our street, a street over, and then another. Whenever I appeared at a door, tanned, with bushy blonde hair, I impressed my neighbors with the rusty old push-mower that glistened from the gallons of oil I slathered over it to keep the gears running and the blades cutting. Nostalgia spread over most of the older folks as they watched me push, the precise staccato of gears and blades reminding them of their youth when everyone had a push-mower. The new spring grass was coming in so there was plenty of work for me to do.

The problem for me was that every lawn kept me from both Laci and the beach. I also collected bottles for the five and ten cent refunds. After two weeks and what seemed like eight hundred lawns and five thousand bottles, I collected a little over one hundred dollars, an enterprising amount for a teenager in 1967.

I learned later that the mayor wanted to give me some kind of award for initiative in urban development. He changed his mind when he learned that the money I earned and all the work I did was for surf camp. When the mayor discovered that, I was just another surf bum.

Between what Mom donated and what Joe put in my hundred or so dollars was more than enough for air fare and the church camp near Makaha.

Laci was not overly happy about the trip, particularly because it meant me going to Hawaii where the big waves lived and played.

The Hobie juniors consisted of Pete Johannsen, Dave Ruffio, Mark Harmond, Eric Murray, Dennis Thompson, Ricky Moon, and me. Dave Ruffio, began surfing when he was six. Like me he had an older brother who taught him things. By the time I started surfing Dave was already in competitions and he was good.

The Hobie t-shirts were psychedelic blue with the Hobie logo on front and back. Knob made the master silk screen for them.

The much anticipated day came upon us, Spring Break, mid-March, 1967. We rose early and loaded the Woody with our bags and surfboards. Half an hour later we collected Denny Thompson and turned toward Malibu where we would meet Hobie and the others at the shop. We drove in a caravan down the coast along with many of the other surf teams.

We were all headed for surfing nirvana—Hawaii. While this would not be Waimea or the North Shore we would probably still see waves larger than anything most of us had ever surfed. We rolled past all the coastal towns and beaches that we had visited and heard about; places like Dana Point, Oceanside, Encino, the Trestles, and La Jolla.

After three hours, we pulled into Lindburgh Field in San Diego with the Woody blowing smoke from a head casket getting ready to go. Besides surfboards and wax, Joe always carried plenty of quarts of motor oil; a '34 Ford Woody was nothing to mess around with, especially with the number of miles Joe and Rod had driven it. There were five surfboards lashed to the top of the Woody: two were Joe's, two were Denny's, and the Spider Woman, which Knob considered his greatest creation, was mine.

Hobie was in charge of the arrangements and the seniors were to act as chaperones for the trip. That was a laugh!

As takeoff approached and our bags and surfboards were loaded onto the airplane, the seniors herded us out onto the tarmac. When we caught sight of our airplane, we stopped and stared in horror. Our plane was not a jet but an old 1950s Constellation, the kind made famous in spectacular crashes in places like the Grand Canyon and the middle of New York City. I couldn't recall any history of a Constellation going down in the ocean so the whole idea was perfect. Inside, the cabin was old and narrow. Its seats were cramped, made for little kids of the 1950s. For us juniors, aside from the little problem of historical mishaps, the environment was perfect. We could make mayhem at close quarters and not be far at all from the pretty stewardesses.

Our takeoff was smooth and the stewardesses were efficient. They explained where the exits were and told us that if the plane made a "water landing" we could rip off the seat cushions as spurious floatation devices. After that we would be on our own. Then they proceeded to tell us about the sinking of the U.S.S. Indianapolis during the Second World War and the worst shark attack in history.

We pondered that.

The seniors quickly disappeared to the forward section of the airplane followed by the stewardesses who were all in their early to mid-twenties. That was okay with the juniors because the pillow fight that began lasted almost seven hours. Though the air was clear at twenty-five thousand feet that day, the pilots both complained of unforeseen turbulence.

When the stewardesses returned to our section to count the dead and clean up, we were all exhausted and half-asleep or dazed in our seats. The stewardesses were all smiles; little angels all.

It wasn't until food was served that the trouble started. Mashed potatoes were the worst offenders. They could fly through the air as an amorphous lump hit the side of a head or splatter and stick sickeningly to the window. Peas and carrots were added for color. I managed to wolf down my chicken before the first barrage began and managed a good hit on a kid from Newport Beach. He scraped a glob of potatoes off his window, turned and fired at me.

Unfortunately, the head stewardess stepped from behind the forward cabin curtain and took it right in her feminine glory.

She was not amused.

In general, stewardesses are intended to make an airplane trip more pleasurable by utilizing their pleasant faces and feminine forms, stylish uniforms, and immeasurably excellent people skills. Heaven help us if men ever became airline stewardesses. However mashed potatoes splattered across the front of the stylish uniform were not part of the package. The resulting tirade was more than sufficient to bring a surly group of young surfers to attention. If it wasn't for the machismo of teenage boys I'm certain there would have been tears. Instead, there was silence, furtive looks, and fear and trembling at 25,000 feet. One kid mused that if we didn't straighten up the head stewardess might ask the pilot to intentionally crash the airplane.

It would have served us right.

The next hour involved scrubbing, wiping, shining, and mopping. Who would have thought that an airplane carried a wet mop?

After the airplane was restored to its original factory cleanliness we were allowed to sit quietly in our seats and contemplate our misdeeds.

A couple of hours later the pilot alerted us to our pending arrival. I looked out the window and down toward the sea, staring into the bluest blue beyond all reason, the blue of the 'Blue Planet," ultra-blue, the blue of Ty-D-Bol; complete and utter blue.

As we descended, I could see the reefs surrounding the islands and waves, magnificent waves, rolling across them. I felt my pulse quicken. Each of the guys jockeyed for a look out the window and there was much pushing and shoving and excited talk about the surf.

The seat belt light went on and no one returned to his seat. However, the curtain merely rustled and blurs filled the cabin. When the head stewardess opened the curtains, she found a cabin full of seat-belted boys all waiting in wild anticipation for the deplaning and our trip to Makaha on the western shore of Oahu. One of the stewardesses told us that Makaha meant "fierce" or "savage" in the Hawaiian language.

'Fierce or savage' certainly hit a tone with all of us juniors; we were fired up.

As we deplaned and the baggage bins in the plane were opened, a rickety old, yellow school bus pulled up onto the tarmac. Oahu was beautiful. The air was salt-water clean, blown by a breeze. The clouds in the sky were like huge cotton balls billowing in a crown above the Islands. Terminal workers started pulling bags out of the compartments and tossing them onto the ground. We swarmed over them grabbing our own or ones that looked like ours. Shoving and pulling matches ensued but it was all good fun with much laughing until Hobie started shouting at us to get on the bus.

Dozens of surfboards were tied to the top of the bus, until it looked like a salvage truck. We boarded, excited to see the waves. The drive to the church camp was up H-5, a two lane road of some disrepair, volcanic cliff on one side and the blue Pacific on the other. The ocean side of the bus was overloaded as guys even stood in the aisle to take a look. After two hours everyone sat down and settled into the chatter of surfers.

Joe was surrounded by his friends as well as many of the juniors who admired him and wanted to listen to his surfing stories. Many of them told me they thought that one day Joe would be a world champion. I smiled at that and agreed with them.

The church camp looked nice, just the right amount of neatness in intent and disorder from the wild.

As we jumped off the bus there were several more Hawaiian girls loaded up with flower wreathes that I learned were called "leis," a Hawaiian tradition that comes along with a kiss. I found myself standing in front of a bronze goddess with Joe directly behind me.

"Aloha," she said sweetly as she slipped the lei over my head and kissed me on the cheek. I suddenly felt a little light-headed but Joe pushed me forward.

As I turned, I saw the girl stare at Joe for a moment and then smile warmly. Joe returned the smile with a grin.

"Aloha," she breathed and slipped the lei over his head. When she leaned forward to kiss him on the cheek, he turned and his lips brushed hers.

"Come on, Joe," one of the other guys shouted from down the line, "Get a room!"

Joe laughed and moved on as the girl's eyes followed his movement. I could almost see the wheels turning in her head.

The cabins they put us in were old barracks left over from World War II, but they were clean and spacious.

The first thing we did after dropping off our bags was eat lunch. The chow hut was cool. The girls who welcomed us actually worked at the camp; they were all there in the serving line and in the kitchen. It only took two seconds for Joe to find the girl we met when we arrived.

I walked up as they were shaking hands,

"Joe Connors," Joe was saying as he held her hand. He glanced at me.

"He's going to become the World Champion," I said, failing to hide my pride in my brother.

The girl smiled and raised her eyebrows.

"World Champion?" she replied sweetly, "There's something we don't see around here every day!" There was a tinge of sarcasm in her tone.

Joe smiled and nearly blushed.

"I'm Lelani," she said, taking my hand.

"Lelani?" I asked releasing her hand, "You have a last name?"

She smiled more broadly.

"It's Hawaiian, you couldn't pronounce it."

"Come on," I challenged, "Try me.

Lelani laughed, "Okay, it's Kahini Mokoe Hulikohola Kahanamoku."

I stared at her for a moment and then turned and moved into the lunch line.

Lelani laughed again, "I told you!"

The food was great, homemade and Hawaiian. I knew it was going to be a great week.

Our ride to the North Shore where we were to visit took us through massive fields of pineapple and sugar cane. The sun was bright and the sky clear; the air was salt-sweet as we arrived at the Pipeline.

For some reason the sea was more massive here than at home. It was a different color too, a deep, resonant blue with whitewater like an avalanche of virgin snow; and the roar sounded like I imagined an avalanche would, thunderous and monumental.

We knew the contest wouldn't be held here; if it had, it would be a contest of survival, kids against mountains. Still, the sight of the massive, perfect, barrels excited even the most timid among us and I knew that Joe would ride them one day. He might not tame them but ride them as if he were born to it.

Because he was.

The wind off the North Shore was nothing like I'd ever felt. It roared in from the west and one or two gusts nearly took the boards off the top of the bus. One gust nearly took the bus.

There were a large number of people there, mostly locals with mainlanders, "haoles," pronounced "howeys" as they were known in the local parlance.

"How do you surf?"

Out on the water it was a little like a scourge of white locusts or a cotton candy machine on steroids; white water spray lifted off the tops of the waves like a blizzard and millions of tons of water spilled over the top of each monstrous wave, rushing down into the momentary troughs below. Everything was deep blue with white spray under a portion of the sky dark and dangerous. It was the moisture of tens of millions of years rising and falling long before those islands sprouted up from the depths. It was the water that gave life; untold millions of marine animals from the lowliest mollusk to the great sperm whales that visited every year. And the islands were filled with life as well; lush green overtaking the mineral-laden volcanic soil at every turn. It was fields of sugar cane and pineapple, stands of macadamia nuts and bananas that tried to make sense of the verdant green chaos creating a perpetual though pathetic attempt by humankind to make its mark. Left alone for a year the jungle would reclaim it all, right down to the shore by the sea.

Our group went out to the beach; most of the older boys carrying their sticks while less of the juniors could muster the courage.

I thought about the short-board but one look at the waves told me that I'd have to play in the kiddie pool just to survive. The "kiddie pool was the name we gave to those areas to the left and the right of the Pipeline. The kiddie pool was bad enough, twice the size that we were used to, with waves roaring in set after set.

Immediately Joe and the other seniors introduced themselves to some of the hardcore wave-riders there. They knew the area because some had grown up here while others had left the mainland to come here and search for the perfect wave.

From what I could see perfect waves were lined up way out in the water waiting for their chance to be king for three minutes and rule the planet.

To my utter disbelief Joe took his longboard, shook some hands, and headed out into the water. My dreams of my brother becoming world champion suddenly grew dim. Joe was good but this was life-or-death stuff, grim-reaper stuff, the stuff of the apocalypse in biblical proportions.

Moses and the Red Sea had it easy compared to the challenge Joe was facing. I was sure he was going to die.

I waited breathlessly for several minutes.

"Worried?" a voice behind me asked.

I looked around and saw Herbie Torres standing there with his board.

I nodded.

Herbie grinned, "No reason to be. Someday Joe Connors is going to rule the world!"

Suddenly all the people around me began standing up and looking out toward the Pipeline.

I gasped as I saw Joe's distinctive navy blue, Hawaiian print beachcombers flying down the face of the tsunami. I found it hard to breathe as he turned and changed his angle. Like it was made just for him, the wave broke over the top and rolled into a magnificent, mind-bending tube; a pipeline the size of a big city water conduit.

I could see Joe riding the lip of the barrel, knees bent, arms outstretched, his trailing hand carving the back of the tube. If I had a movie camera and could have filmed it I would play it back in slow motion and find that it was perfect—a grand ballet of grace and incalculable power.

When the tube crashed, sending white water like a bomb rending the earth, I knew then that my brother had bought it. As I continued to watch I tried to imagine our mother's reaction. "It was terrible, Mom, the ocean just ate him, crushed him like a grape for new wine."

The sudden applause brought me back from my macabre revelry. Looking out I saw my brother, Joe Connors riding through the white water, arms raised above his head like a prize fighter in triumph. And it had been a fight.

"You were right," a softer voice said. I turned to see Lelani and some of the other girls from the camp applauding loudly. "He is going to be a world champion someday."

She smiled, winked, and gave me the 'hang ten' sign.

We took turns out on the waves, me on the outside and Herbie right up the middle. It was unbelievable to watch him, a small form out on a massive mountain, almost like a skier riding the side of the Alps.

His wipeout was the stuff of legend; turning slightly too forward coming off the lip. The nose caught and he was launched into space. It turned out to be a lot like jumping off the top of a three-story building and then having the building fall on you. Lifeguards paddled furiously knowing that a first time rider falls at great risk.

Several of the lifeguards dove deep into the rising swells. In a minute or two they dragged out a nearly lifeless Herbie Torres. It turned out that he was okay but he had the wind knocked out of him and the water packed in.

"Herbie!" I hollered as I ran over to where he was stretched out on the sand, "Are you okay, Dude?"

He coughed and nodded.

"That wipe-out was awesome," another one of the kids blurted as he ran up. "Awesome!"

Herbie coughed again and nodded.

"Yeah," he gasped, trying to catch his breath, "Gnarly. You've got to try it!"

The kid's eyes went wide and he nodded warily.

The sun and the wind ruled the day like the ancient Hawaiian kings and queens.

It could not have been better for my brother's reputation as it grew to almost instant legend; he rode the biggest, meanest, and the most awesome waves I'd ever seen.

The stories I could tell when I returned to the mainland, and I wouldn't even have to embellish. I could write poems about his feats. How much bigger could it be?

Our return to church camp was triumphant. We felt like Caesars returning on golden chariots; in our case, a rusty and yellow school bus. The talk was about the guys who rode the Pipeline. We talked about Herbie, who was either the only junior with guts or else the one with the lowest IQ. And of course we talked about Joe. Five of the seniors actually made the ride, but Joe rode it a half-dozen times, each time with more style and speed than the last.

When we arrived at the camp most of the surfers headed for the showers to get the brine out of their hair and off their skin .

Joe walked straight to the chow hut and I had a bet it wasn't because he wanted dinner. He was looking for Lelani.

That night a huge bonfire blazed and a band of locals played surf music, as well as all kinds of wild Polynesian music. Several large locals came out into the firelight and danced with flaming torches. It was awesome; the drums, the dances, the torches!

I saw Joe and Lelani walking hand-in-hand, not far from the bonfire. Joe must have been telling Lelani about his everything paper and I'll bet she was impressed. I know I was even if I didn't understand what Joe was talking about.

I sat with Herbie and some of the other juniors, watching the dancers, the camp girls, the blazing fire, and watching the camp girls some more.

Everyone told their stories and their lies from the day. One thing, however, is that there were no embellishments to be done about those who rode the Pipeline. The thing was too big; either you rode it or you didn't. Or you might be whacked by it like Herbie Torres was. What was strange was that Herbie's failure was far-better than our best successes. If we wiped out in the kiddy pool, we only wiped out on a ten-foot drop; for Herbie, it was a drop into legend, or nearly so.

Time and time again the conversation would drift around to Joe and all eyes would fall on me. And though I wasn't Joe, I knew him in the depths; I was blood, and I was his only brother.

I let them all talk because as a wise old man in Pacific Palisades, Father Bernardo, once told me, "If you've done it, it ain't bragging." No one could argue that Joe Connors had done it. And Joe had done it big time.

There was talk that maybe Joe should stay in the Islands, go pro, and ride the Pipe Masters. I knew he wouldn't do it, not now anyway, not with Rod joining the Marines and going to boot camp. Joe had to be there, maybe out of a little guilt that he wasn't also going, but knew, or thought he knew, that his destiny lay elsewhere. There was that, and there was still school.

Still, everyone knew that he would do it one day because he was a natural.

I excused myself to go to the Little Boy's Room, and as I stepped out of the firelight the light of the full moon took over. I could see two figures, Joe and Lelani—standing out under a tree. Their faces were very close together when suddenly Joe kissed her and she kissed him back. I froze in my tracks because thoughts of the girl I left behind came rushing back to me. Would I kiss Laci like that someday, deeply and for what would seem like hours? I shook it off and ran to the restroom.

The Makaha began in less than twelve hours.

Chapter Three

The sun rose and the air in the church camp was filled with excitement and anticipation. We'd all been in contests before, but this was the first time for many of us to be in a contest so far from home. It was a preview of what the pro-circuit would be like.

Surfers lived paradoxical lives, their activities took them to high and dangerous places on the tops of waves, then sent them down at break-neck speeds; yet when out of the water, they were the most laid-back people. Often their movements were slow and graceful, their speech languid. It was this paradox that confused people who did not surf, people who did not live in the sea or visit the Green Room. The surfer knew the sea gave life and could give the greatest of waves and, just as easily, take them away in an instant.

We loaded our surf boards onto the bus. As we climbed aboard the bus our thoughts were focused on the task ahead. The excitement and rising pressure kept most of us fairly quiet. Now, as we looked around the bus at one another we wondered who would wipe out and who would prevail? Most eyes worked their way toward my brother.

"He's got it," Herbie Torres said quietly, almost reverently. "Joe is a surfer dude, Dude!"

Then he smiled and returned to his own reverie.

About twenty minutes later the blue water came into view; the Big Blue, the ocean where great and terrible things had happened. A whole people from Polynesia rowed their way across unimaginable weeks of blue before arriving at these islands. How did they navigate, how did they even know of the islands?

There had been great, world-shaking battles here in this blue, and men, sent up into outer space came down and were recovered here.

Makaha Beach Park was alive with people. There were banners, balloons, food vendors, life guards, a medical tent, and crowd stands. Overseeing everything was a judges' booth with a big, blank, white leader-board directly behind it.

It was almost a carnival atmosphere except surfers did not think of themselves as clowns or entertainers. Most did it for the love of the waves. When they competed it was only to see who was best.

The huge loudspeakers were blaring with music from a local band. Rock 'n roll was pounding the sand and could be felt in the toes. The group began to play the Dick Dale and the Del Tones' hit, "King of the Surf Guitar." Most of us didn't mind that song though we really didn't like the other bands that romanticized surfing. Bands like Jan and Dean or the Beach Boys, didn't really surf; although Dennis Wilson, the drummer for the Beach Boys, did surf a little. They were musicians and didn't really understand the soul of the surfer.

Dick Dale was a real surfer.

Standing at the edge of the water we could see that Makaha was alive too. It wasn't ferocious like the North Shore, but Makaha had long, peeling rights. During the big swells we could see bowls and the swells generally came from the north and the west. The result, of course, was a backwash that either returned as a riptide or as an undertow depending on the size of the swell. Either way, we knew a surfer had to be careful, read the signs, and know how to handle the situation as it changed.

We lined up for registration and looking around I saw a contestants-only area where there seemed to be food and drink. That was nice. Most of our contests at home required that we bring a sandwich or a hot dog and if we forgot we had it in our pockets and hit the waves it was a long, hungry day.

The beach thick with all kinds of girls, the kinds of girls that made a fellow glad he was a surfer. There were even girls who knew how to surf and were very good at it.

Still, there was little recognition internationally for female surfers, though in California some girls were becoming well known, Women like Marge Calhoun, Linda Benson, and Anne Morrissey were becoming better known after becoming Pacific Coast Champions since 1959. The day would come when women surfers would get all the recognition they deserved.

Personally, I wished it was today.

Our names were called and we paddled out into the surf in groups of four. The breeze was blowing off shore at a fairly stiff rate. It wasn't as strong as the North Shore, but I was glad all of the flags, banners, and balloons were anchored tightly.

I saw Lelani standing with Joe, his arm hanging comfortably around her shoulders.

I liked Lelani. She had a kind of no-nonsense look at the world, up-close and personal all the time. She was the kind that Joe liked; the real, grounded, surfer-girl type. She knew the waves and the sticks, the guns, and the lingo. She could tell beach break from reef break and reef break from the real deal, and that said a lot.

The waves were running a good ten to twelve feet; calm compared to the winter when the conditions were described a ferocious In the winter Makaha was more like the North Shore with fierce waves slamming the coast at fifteen to thirty feet high. The winter brought vicious riptides ready to tear a surfer and board in half.

I hated riptides because they were a waste of time and sometimes dangerous. You'd get caught in one and would have to battle perpendicular for who knew how long to get out of it. My worst nightmare was getting caught in one that I'd have to paddle to Mexico to get out of! If you went over the falls into one the undertow might drag you out to a sea drowning.

Riptides are one of the reasons that surfers began using the ankle cord. If a surfer wiped out and drowned the board would indicate where the body was and a perfectly good board would not be wasted.

Dead man's board.

My group consisted of Tommy Stevens who was a Jacobs kid, and two locals—Stewart and Kaipo. Stewart was from Oahu and Kaipo from up near the North Shore of Maui. Kaipo was hardcore.

We paddled out into the lineup, watching as the group in front took off in the order they were drawn.

The two locals were interested in my shortboard, especially the artwork, but Stevens just scoffed at it. The two locals looked at him and began laughing.

"Dude," Kaipo said, "The shortboard is the future, man. They can slice and carve and fly, I've seen it."

"Shortboards are going to mean points in the future," Stewart added, "Maybe even today!"

They both winked at Stevens while he returned that typical Jacobs-team scowl.

Kaipo was first up. He shoved his board around as we all rose with the swell. He began paddling and caught the wave cleanly; beauteously in fact. Down he went over the lip, carving down the face a little with his big gun. It must have looked good because the crowd was cheering on shore.

Stevens went next, paddling in long, even strokes, catching the wave and disappearing from sight. I could tell from where I was sitting that the wave was rolling and Stevens was hunkered down in Emerald, Orin this case, the Coral Blue City.

The crowd began to cheer as he rode toward the mouth trying to get out front. Suddenly, the crowd stopped cheering and about four lifeguards ran for the water.

Chicken Little was right, the Sky Room had fallen in and Stevens had gone down in the white water.

He was okay though. He'd had a good ride in the barrel that lasted until the roof caved in. The lifeguards were just out there making sure he was all right.

My turn was next, but Stewart and I waited through a swell until Stevens was out of sight on the beach. I could see the next group of juniors paddling outside to get up into the lineup behind us.

The next swell began to rise and I turned back to see Stewart give me the thumbs-up sign.

"Go, Bra!" he shouted with a big smile on his brown face.

I could feel the wave giving life, rising up to head for the break. I paddled furiously and caught it just as it began to break over the top.

I jumped to my feet and quickly gained my footing.

As the barrel began to form, I changed my angle to stay out in front of it across the face. The crowd seemed perplexed. It wasn't something that I would normally do but I wanted to score some points with my shortboard. Up I flew toward the lip, the barrel roaring behind me like a leviathan.

I was glad I didn't have time to think about it because the very thought would have wiped me out.

Instead, I broke over the lip, executed a one-eighty and flew back down, only to turn and try it again. When I broke the lip this time, I could Stewart with his hands on his head in near hysteria. Joe had worked hard to teach me how to fly with the shortboard and it was payback time.

I caught the lip again, grabbed the nose and turned another one-eighty, flying, truly flying as my feet lifted off the board. When I landed, I carved down and up, down and up, before turning to leave the collapsing barrel behind.

The white water exploded around me and I had made my point—Spider Woman could fly and the short board was on its way!

After the first round I was in first place, impressing the judges with the aerial. I believed that by staying up in the white water I might have a few more points to cushion the second day.

"Hey Bro," Joe said as he came up and wrapped his arms around me in a big bear hug. Lelani did the same thing and I admit that I liked her's better. There's a limit on brotherly love, or so I thought.

The seniors went out and Joe rode them all down. He was spectacular, riding the barrel so deep that we all thought he had disappeared in some kind of time warp. He literally wrote "J-O-E," across the face and blew the lip as the wave collapsed going down the back side and riding in on yet another wave. It had to be one of the longest surf rides in history and left him standing atop the leader board at the end of Day One.

Most of us were exhausted by the time we climbed onto the bus and fell into the seats. We made our way back to the church camp. Dinner was great; roasted pork, pineapple, all kinds of stuff both familiar and new. There was a great deal of smiling and eye-batting from the camp girls. Apparently they didn't mind where their heroes came from! Hero-worship was in the air. Of course, we weren't really heroes. We might put our lives on the line but never for some great cause as do soldiers, firemen, or policemen. One thing was for certain, the Connors brothers were on top of the surfing world at that moment.

As much as most of us wanted to sleep, the locals were not having any of it; they could not let the day go without a celebration.

The same band that played out at the beach was there for the party. They gave way to the thunder of Hawaiian drums as some large locals came out and began dancing with ancient Hawaiian hammers or swords or something equally lethal. A couple had fiery torches tossing them around a bit too flippantly for my tastes. They dragged me and Joe out to the middle of the circle and danced flames around us. A couple of times I thought of the headlines: "Mainland Brothers Immolated in Fiery Fertility Dance!" I knew if the dancers came much closer I'd end up looking like Knob, which wouldn't be all that bad if I could get his art skills too.

Suddenly they stopped, frozen in their tracks as two wahinis stepped forward. Lelani and another camp girl placed crowns made of grass or some kind of heavy vegetation upon our heads. The crowd burst into wild applause and Lelani told us that we were now members of the warrior class. I was nearly knocked to the ground several times by happy Hawaiian brothers clapping me on the back.

We were kings for the day.

The revelry lasted well past midnight before some of the boys started drifting off to their bunks.

I collapsed into mine, shut my eyes, and was in a dream in seconds. I wondered what Laci would think of my crown, and would she be my queen, if only for a day?

The second and final day of the Makaha Invitational at Makaha Beach Park was even more glorious than the first; the Sun dominated the cloudless, diamond blue sky. The crystal blue water broke into barrel after barrel, the white water painting a tapestry of spray.

We remained in the same foursome as the day before. As we walked past the television camera behind the announcer we heard him say, "And yesterday was dominated by the Connors brothers of Team Hobie out of Malibu, California."

The Connors brothers; I liked that.

Kaipo and Stewart both grinned and slapped me on the shoulder.

"The *Connors* brothers," Kaipo repeated with a laugh, "You Haoles are too cool!"

Stevens just grunted, but he nodded his head.

We began paddling to the outside as we watched the group ahead of us braving the wild surf; catching a wave, the greatest sport around.

A couple of bad wipe-outs had the rest of us already thinking; while the conditions appeared to be the same as the day before, there was something in the wind, a challenge or an unwillingness to give up the ride.

When we took our place in the lineup, I sensed menace in the swells. They seemed like the same swells, but there was something dark in them and I couldn't put my finger on it.

Suddenly, Kaipo turned his face toward me with a look of concern.

"Lono ain't happy, Bra," he said loudly.

I looked around, "Lono?" I replied, "Who's Lono?"

"Surf god," he shouted, "coming down to crash the party!"

Stewart nodded and shouted, "We'd better get on with it then!"

Stevens looked as confused as I was.

Immediately Kaipo took off as the sea began to swell. He caught the wave and leaned over the lip into a fifteen-foot drop as the wave somehow tucked itself in. I saw the board and Kaipo flying upside down into the white water.

We waited as the lifeguards inched forward toward the water. A minute later Kaipo climbed onto his board and paddled his way in.

Stevens looked at me with a little more than concern on his face.

"Man," he said as he shook his head.

"Go, Bra," Stewart shouted, "Watch the break!"

Stevens caught the wave, stood up on the lip and then tried to bail.

The bottom was gone again and in a second, so was Stevens. He hit the bottom, disappeared into the white water and the mountain fell down on him.

"Dude," Stewart cried, "We've got to catch the lip a second later, let it make up its mind. Like holding off on an off-speed pitch."

Every kid knew what that was, even surfer kids.

Stevens made it to shore okay and I watched as the sea rose around me. Off to my right another foursome was trying to make its way to the lineup, moving slowly probably waiting to see what I was going to do.

"Go, Bra," Stewart shouted, "Give it a second!"

I paddled, watched the wave begin to break, hesitated a moment, then charged over the lip.

I lay on the board, kept my nose up, and made it down onto the face. I crouched as the barrel rolled open and ran my hand across the back of it. I wanted to get out for an aerial but something told me to hold. Just as the ceiling caved in, I angled downward trying to out run the many tons of blue. Once outside I tried to carve up, hit the remaining lip on the outside, grabbed the nose of my short board, and spun. As I came around fully, there was nothing! I held onto my board with one hand trying to use it as a parachute or at least keep the board with me when they found my body. When it hit the exploding white water I pushed the board down and landed on it, rode it for a moment or two, until the remaining water swept me off my feet and into the air like a pogo stick. Spider Woman, the pogo stick.

How many points for a magnificent, uncontrolled aerial I wondered as I hit the water. When I opened my eyes I'd almost landed face-first on the bottom.

"Ouch!" I hoped I would still look presentable with my nose scraped off. Would Laci go for a noseless boyfriend? I rolled, feet over head and launched myself off the bottom, my face barely missing the ocean floor.

I was still alive and ready to surf.

As I paddled toward the shore, I could see the crowd applauding and, as my ears cleared of seawater, I could hear them. Maybe the locals weren't as fascinated with train wrecks as we were on the Mainland; maybe they were cheering the fact that I was still alive!

I looked over my shoulder to see Stewart heading for the barrel. He was playing it safe just trying to stay up.

When I pulled myself onto shore a crowd gathered around. They were excited and all talking at once.

"Never seen anything like it, Dude!"

"Awesome!"

"How did you do that, Man?"

I was a little confused at first but then the judges points came up and the crowd erupted again.

Herbie and Hobie were both on me in a second.

"What guts, Kid," Hobie said as he clapped me on the back, "The short board is going to go nuts."

I saw Stewart carrying his stick up out of the water.

"I am telling you, Man, nobody does that in this water!" Herbie said with uncharacteristic excitement

I smiled but was still battling confusion when Stewart walked up with Kaipo and Stevens.

"Everybody rides the barrel, Bra," Stewart said, "Today it is safe play, but you…"

"Lono smiled on you, Bra," Kaipo added.

Stevens held out his hand, "Great job, Man," he said sincerely.

Suddenly, I was lifted off the sand in a great bear hug. It was one of my warrior "brothers."

"Little brother," the giant man grunted, "You almost surf like an Islander!"

When he released me nearly knocking me to the ground with a slap on the back, another bear hug came from my big brother and his Amazon Hawaiian wahini Lelani.

The moment was mine.

All of the congratulating and partying kept us distracted and we didn't see the clouds move in, casting a dark shroud over the water.

I was done for the day, three rides with a good lead. I had to wait until the last junior was in to see if I still stood tall.

For the seniors, however, it was going to get messy and nasty very quickly. Lono, the surf god, was looking for some payback for us juniors presuming to surf and not showing enough respect. One of my warrior "brothers" walked up and put a huge arm on my shoulder.

"Looks like we are going to have to sacrifice someone, Bra," he said solemnly shaking his head, "In the old days, if you were king or chief, it was the winner that was sacrificed."

I looked up at him in shock.

"Yea, Lono is angry," he continued, sliding his arm across onto my other shoulder, "Needs appeasing, someone who presumes to be the winner."

I stepped away from my "brother."

"Wait a minute," I stammered, trying to think. "There wasn't anything like this in the travel brochure!"

"Of course not," the brother said, spreading his hands as if to apologize, "Would you come if you knew you might be sacrificed?"

"Wait, wait!" I said, "How about sacrificing a virgin or something? Everybody sacrifices virgins."

The big bronze brute thought about it for a moment.

"I wish I could help you, Bra," he said as the corner of his mouth began to rise.

"What wrong with sacrificing a virgin?" I asked nearing panic.

"Because, Bra," he smiled and then leaned toward me, "There are no virgins in Hawaii."

I immediately took off running as the big man lunged at me.

He took a few steps and stopped as Joe and Lelani walked up.

The big man roared with laughter.

"What's so funny, Bro?" Joe asked as he turned to watch me escape with my life.

The big man bent over and picked up my board, setting it upright in the sand.

"I told little brother that in the old days when Lono was angry they usually sacrificed the best surfer, the winner."

Lelani was horrified.

"You did not!" she cried, "You want him to think that we're savages?"

"He wanted to sacrifice virgins," the big man replied with a chuckle, "Now that's savagery!"

Lelani crossed her arms and glared at the big man.

"And what did you tell him, Marcus?" she asked, growing suspicious.

"That there were no virgins in Hawaii..." He broke into a run with Lelani on his tail.

"No thanks to you, Marcus Hanakona!" Lelani shouted, scooping up sand and throwing it as she ran.

I didn't realize that at that moment the last junior made it in. I'd won my first surfing contest by three points. I was still on the run.

Things were about to happen quickly. The seniors, charged into the surf.

The wind picked up, kicking the waves even higher making them less stable. The seniors began running, fighting the untamed water. Of course most of them were up to the challenge—they were bigger and stronger than the juniors. Rider after rider hunkered down into the barrel and rode it out. The better riders, or the lucky ones, stayed up in the white water riding in triumphantly like the Caesars of ancient Rome on their chariots.

Joe's first ride was much the same as everyone else's. He jumped off the lip, angled down and settled perfectly into the Green Room, which actually became green as the waves rose. We were starting to get deep water from the storm out at sea.

His second ride took him clean out of the barrel; he carved up and then down, riding at incredible speed. Any faster and he would be going into a time warp.

The crowd loved it and his point total began to grow.

The rain hit like a curtain and everyone but the surfers and those dressed for the beach began scrambling for cover.

It was a warm shower and actually felt good!

ROBERT CURTIS

Chapter Four

Joe was all soul on the water. He'd sit on his board and watch and feel.

"This is what it's all about, Bro," he told me as we sat on our boards off Makaha, rising and falling with the swells. "There was this storm off Jakarta, typhoon-like, hairy. And it started the waves moving, rolling in sets."

I glanced at the incoming set as they rolled toward us. They weren't North Shore but they were still real beauties.

"That was three days ago, Bro," Joe continued, looking off into the distance. His mind was in the sea and sun. "And now we get them from a couple of thousands of miles away."

He grinned that big, toothy grin and immediately turned, stroking for the inside. I watched, still fascinated after all this time. Joe caught the wave like the artist he was, cleanly, and then he rose majestically like a Hawaiian god. His tan was deep enough to appear Hawaiian though his shining blonde locks flew around behind him instead of the ink black of Polynesia. That in itself, would have made him a god in the ancient days in the Islands. He turned down along the face; a good wave rose ten, maybe even fifteen feet.

The wave was just a form moving through the mass of the water, a whole bundle of energy drawing itself out in a curve. But the shoaling sandbar out in front of the bowl wouldn't let the curve keep its shape. All that energy tumbled higher and tighter until it reached up over itself, and created the wave form yet again, Then it forced water out to close the curve, but with a hollow spinning core.

When Joe dipped down he physically entered the heart of the ocean's energy.

No other activity did that, no sport penetrated the heart; nothing brought you closer to the Earth. It's the ultimate reality show called the tube, the barrel, the pipeline, the Green Room. It's the Emerald City in the Land of Oz.

I felt one rise under me and immediately set out for the inside. I stroked furiously as I suddenly realized I was late on the take-off. When the wave broke, I had to accept the inevitable and it was over the falls, kicking myself on the way down.

When I came ashore I was glad that the contest was already over.

Of course Joe won the senior prize. I won my first junior division trophy. Joe was happier for me than he was for himself. I had to admit that winning the Makaha Invite wasn't bad considering I beat the young Hawaiian guys who were born on a board. They were nothing but cool in my mind; called me their best "haole," which I understood to be a heavy compliment in these parts.

That night at the awards ceremony a large bonfire and several smaller fires blazed in the area of the beach where everyone gathered. There were many more people there than I'd expected. Most of the crowd were locals dressed in traditional Hawaiian costumes, some wore grass skirts. Others wore the brightly-colored cotton prints that were becoming popular in California. The rest of us looked like vagrants but the locals never seemed to care; they treated everyone in the same friendly manner.

Hobie Alder and one of the local organizers stepped up to a microphone which was attached to a large, ancient speaker.

"Aloha!" the local organizer, Billy Hook, announced and the crowd responded enthusiastically. Billy was a large man with a smile that almost filled his face.

"Tonight we have a great honor at this, the Sixth Annual Makaha Invitational," he paused for effect and watched the faces of the surfers in the firelight. "To present the awards we have the one and only greatest surfer of all time…"

He let his voice trail off as I suddenly took a deep breath and held it.

"Duke Kohanamoku!" Billy shouted out the name of the surfing legend.

The crowd went wild, especially us boys who had heard the tales of Duke Kohanamoku, or "the Duke" as he was known in surfing circles. Because he lived much of the year in Newport Beach, many of the young surfers had even seen him or met him while he was there.

An elderly, white-haired Hawaiian man dressed in a white cotton shirt and a traditional white cotton Hawaiian skirt walked slowly to the microphone. He was stooped slightly forward and walked with effort, but we could see the perfect athlete underneath.

The Duke was an Olympian for the United States, winning gold and silver in swimming in 1912, and 1920. In 1924 he won a silver medal and in 1932 he appeared with the U.S. Water Polo team. He was an actor too, and had appeared in several Hollywood movies.

Born Duke Paoa Kahinu Mokoe Hulikohola Kahanamoku, he grew up near Waikiki and learned to surf on the ancient boards The wooden boards of the past were called "olo" and made from the wood of the Koa tree. He was the first to bring surfing to the mainland, starting out in Santa Cruz and spreading it up and down the coast in the early 1900's.

None of us used wooden boards as the Duke did, especially the big guns of sixteen feet or more. To us he was the god of surfing.

"Aloha," he said softly into the microphone, and the crowd answered in a more subdued and respectful tone. Somehow I found myself bowing.

When my name was called, I stepped forward to receive my trophy and shake the hand of the Duke.

When Joe's name was called a group of locals went crazy, cheering wildly and chanting something in Hawaiian that I could not make out.

They took their surfing seriously in the Islands.

The Duke handed Joe his sizeable trophy, shook hands with him, and bowed.

"You surf like a wing upon the wind," the Duke said as Joe raised his trophy to the delight of the crowd.

Joe seemed unfazed accepting a trophy and a hand from the man who had one time saved eight fishermen from drowning, Their boat had capsized trying to enter the harbor at Newport Beach during a storm. Duke had rescued them, all on his sixteen foot "olo," cutting through the surf, time and time again. The Newport Beach sheriff later said that the Duke's act was the single greatest life-saving event he had ever witnessed.

Billy Hook closed the ceremony by thanking Hobie and the other sponsors; then he invited everyone to celebrate. The music started, and people began dancing. The Hawaiian cooks opened up the underground steam ovens, called imus, that had been buried in the sand the night before. It was time for the lu'au and the food coming out of the imus was plentiful: kalua pig, lau lau, which was more pig, Ahi Poke, raw, marinated Ahi tuna. In addition there was plenty of poi, salads, soft-drinks and desserts. The locals were famous for their luaus and it showed.

A surfing band was there and they broke into a magnificent rendition of the ever-popular "Pipeline."

I remained awe-struck at the sight of the Duke who had now managed to find a spot around one of the fire pits.

There was also plenty of laughter because when Hawaiians and mainland surfers gathered it was a gathering of kindred spirits. The Hawaiians had come a long way from the tribal days when ferocity was their hallmark. Now, people generally equated them with joy and laughter. But I knew after being with many of them for an entire week, they were just like anyone else—laughter and tears, joy and sorrow.

Suddenly Joe walked up beside me. I noticed immediately that he was holding hands with Lelani.

"Come on, Kid," Joe said as he patted my shoulder, "Lelani wants us to meet someone."

Meet someone? I knew who I wanted to meet and maybe I could before the celebration was over and we had to return home.

I shrugged and followed them.

"Grandpa," Lelani said before I realized where we had gone, "These are the two boys I wanted you to meet. You met them at the ceremony; this is Joe Connors and his brother, Pat."

Before it could register in my numbed brain, my outstretched hand was enveloped by the aged but still firm grip of the legendary Duke Kohanamoku.

"Please sit with us," he said as he motioned to the sand around us. People scooted in every direction to make room and we sat.

The Duke looked directly at Joe and nodded, "Wing on the wind. You surf from your soul."

Joe smiled and replied, "So does my little brother."

The Duke turned his wizened gaze toward me and met my eyes.

"You learn from your brother," he said, a statement more than a question.

I nodded.

I had a lot to learn about surfing and life, but the Duke was one who could teach it.

The party was great, lots of music and food and the presence of the Great Duke Paoa Kahinu Mokoe Hulikohola Kahanamoku, the greatest surfer who ever lived.

The return to the camp was again triumphant. We passed the trophies around and everyone claimed that the next time it would be theirs. It was a great ending to a great surf riding contest. That night Lelani invited Joe and me to go snorkeling off Waikiki. The organizers gave us permission because the next day was a free day; the bus would be going to the beach again, this time down to Maili.

We drove down to Waikiki in the old car that Lelani owned, carrying diving masks, snorkels, and fins with us. We were all set to see the sights, especially considering we had a beautiful and native guide to show us around.

Parking near the beach, we took our gear down to the water. There were quite a few people on the beach, mostly visitors from around the world.

I thought about beach life as we waded into the water; it was very different from other kinds of life on Earth. We saw endless horizons at the beach while people from other places inland saw distant mountains or skyscrapers. The ocean was always moving but a concrete front yard stayed still. As we continued wading we slipped on our fins and hobbled into the surf awkwardly, the way swim fins force you to walk. Once outside the beach break we began to swim, slowly, face into the water and breathing through the snorkel.

Below me I could see the clear, blue kingdom of the sea; Neptune's kingdom, the kingdom of whales and dolphins and all manner of aquatic creatures.

This was truly Poseidon's planet.

I wished I had a camera. The coral reef was beautiful and serene. As surfers Joe and I had an affinity for the sea. Surfers were who we were, surfing was what we did.

Lelani pointed out many things. We saw leopard sharks, tropical fish and whole schools of sardines and anchovies. There were some lobsters and even an octopus, though it wasn't very friendly.

I wanted to see dolphins who I felt were the best surfers in the world. They knew how to swim inside the wave, riding within the heart of the sea. They often rode the wakes of boats and ships just for fun, as if they needed the practice. To see a whole pod of dolphin share a wave was wondrous. If only we could learn such a thing and not fight about it.

I learned about dolphins and whales in school. I also read many books about them on my own. I learned they were as sentient as human beings, just smart enough to stay in the water. I speculated that we were probably the same species at one time. Later those of us who crawled onto land evolved into higher primates, and eventually into human beings. This accounted for the affinity dolphins seem to have with human beings. with countless stories of people being rescued by dolphins. I also thought that dolphins may have lost some of that kinship when we started catching them in tuna nets, drowning them, choking them with our plastic garbage or poisoning them with mercury. I looked at a dead cetacean almost as sadly as I looked at dead *homo sapiens*, with grief and the sadness of loss.

Time always moved too quickly in the water, time clocks or rising tides always calling us back to dry land.

Why were we made of so much water? Why was our blood salty?

I asked Lelani about her family as we walked out of the water and onto the beach.

She told me her family was directly descended from kings, most notably from King Kamehameha.

I looked at her for a moment as we dried off and put the snorkeling equipment into the trunk of her car.

"I meant your family now," I said with surprise, "You're an Hawaiian princess?"

"In the flesh," she replied nonchalantly. I didn't know that when you asked an Hawaiian about their family, that lineage was everything. To ask about one's family in Hawaii meant to ask about the whole history.

"My grandfather was a chief and my mother was daughter to a chief," she said. "That's my story and I am sticking to it."

I had to laugh as Joe wrapped his arm around her.

"My parents are both gone," she said wistfully. "I lived with my grandmother before she passed away last year. I have no close family but half of Oahu is related to me."

I marveled at the paradox.

The next day we boarded our bus with all our boards and luggage.

Lelani tried not to cry, but the way she kissed Joe said it all. She promised that she would come to the World Cup at Doheny Beach to be held in December. Joe said he would make the arrangements.

Many of us left with cheerful tears; many of the camp girls cried as well. I must have been oblivious to everyone but Joe and Lelani. Friendships had developed between other couples but I never noticed until the moment we were leaving.

Our flight home was eventless, not even a dollop of mashed potatoes across the aisle. The trip ended the most exciting thing that many of us juniors had ever experienced.

Mom was there to greet us at the airport and she was genuinely happy to see us. I think she was a little relieved to see us, too.

Home was still home.

Joe and Rod had a week to sew things up, tell the stories, and surf the waves together.

Joe did not forget about Lelani. He told mom all about her and he drew some pictures of her. Besides being a great surfer Joe was also a fairly good artist.

On Saturday evening, we had a big going-away party for Rod at his house. His father cooked a ton of hamburgers and hot dogs. There were chips, beans, and sodas, and all his friends to share the evening. The spring of 1967 was a wonderful time.

Chapter Five

The next evening, at around six o'clock, we headed over to Rod's house and drove him and his father to the bus depot. We waited with the two of them.

"What's it like when you first arrive at boot camp?' I asked Dave.

Dave smiled slightly.

"Rough," he replied, "But it's supposed to be rough. The whole purpose is to break you down as an individual and build you back up as a Marine, part of the Corps."

I gazed intently at him.

"What do they do when you first get there?"

"A DI storms onto the bus and tells everyone they have about ten seconds to get off HIS bus!" Rod replied with a serious expression on his face.

"They spend the first nights trying to disorient you, playing mind games, so that you can't think on your own," he added.

"What's a 'DI'?" I asked curiously. My Marine Corps knowledge was practically non-existent.

"Drill Instructor," Dave replied. "I was a DI for ten years. Break 'em down and build 'em back up. Turn high school graduates into killing machines."

I looked at Dave shocked at the idea he'd trained killing machines. "Killing machines?"

Dave nodded solemnly. "Marines have the toughest job of all," he replied, "First to fight, Semper Fi!"

"What does that mean?" I asked feeling like I was in class again.

"Always Faithful," Rod said, "Faithful to yourself, the Creed, the Corps, and the Flag. Not always in that in that order."

I wondered about this Marine Corps' thing.

"What makes the Marine Corps different from the rest of the military?" I asked, becoming more interested in this branch of the service.

"Every Marine is a rifleman," Dave replied, "Cooks, jeep drivers, generals, and all officers. Even jet pilots are trained first as riflemen. And Tarawa makes them different. So do places like Iwo Jima and Okinawa."

I'd heard about Iwo Jima, a volcanic chunk of rock south of the Japanese Islands. It had been good for absolutely nothing but landing bombers on. The month-long battle for Iwo Jima cost the Japanese nearly all of the 22,000 men defending the island against the Marine amphibious assault. It cost us nearly as many in dead and wounded. But the Marines won and bombers landed there. From Iwo Jima they flew on to bomb Japan. Iwo Jima won the war as did other battles on other Pacific islands. Iwo Jima was where the Marines raised the flag in a famous photograph that inspired the war-weary nation.

The bus bound for San Diego pulled into the terminal and opened its doors. People coming to Los Angeles disembarked and headed out to spread throughout the city. But I saw other boys around the same age as Rod and Joe, standing around looking nervous, trying to get rid of their folks so they could move into manhood. Most were anxious for their challenge though not everyone was sure-fire excited about combat. Rod rose and took hold of his very small bag.

"Well, Dad," he said to Dave, "This is it."

Dave gazed at him with a distinct look of pride.

Joe stepped forward and held out his hand.

"You'll join after me," Rod said with a smile, "And maybe we'll meet up in 'Nam; go surfing off the coast."

Joe smiled. "Vietnam doesn't have anything worth surfing, just pathetic beach break" he said, "Give me another reason to go."

Rod shook his head and laughed.

He turned and nodded at me and Laci. Then he turned and hugged his father Dave seemed the slightest bit uncomfortable at the display of affection.

Rod boarded with the other young men and we waved good-bye as the bus pulled away. We would see Rod two more times.

Dave's eyes watered and he wiped at them slowly.

"I hate this pollution," he muttered as he dabbed the corners of his eyes with his handkerchief. "Bothers my allergies."

We all nodded in agreement. We knew Dave was both proud of his son and a little sad to see him leave. I didn't consider that he was probably more than a little frightened for him as well.

The bus drove down through the gates of the Marine Corps Recruit Depot just off I-5 in San Diego, California. Rod sat in the first window seat on the door side of the bus, staring out into the surrounding city lights. The bus was almost full and everyone on it looked either scared or bemused. Rod was sure the latter would soon fade away. Rod remembered what his Dad told him about what to expect, and when the bus pulled to a stop in what looked like a parking lot, he was poised and ready to jump.

Suddenly, the doors flew open. A short, extraordinarily crisp-looking Marine DI, wearing a campaign hat and a look that had probably already killed, stepped up into the aisle of the bus.

"You pukes have ten seconds to get the hell off MY bus!" he roared.

Rod was first off the bus, not waiting for the maelstrom behind him. He was first past the screaming junior drill instructors and first to plant his shoes on the yellow footprints painted lovingly on the asphalt.

A junior DI flew into his face.

"You think you're a smart boy for standing on my parade grounds?" the young Marine NCO shouted.

"No, drill instructor," Rod shouted back at the top of his lungs, "The Recruit is not a smart boy!"

The junior DI paused at the response and brought his nose closer to Rod's.

"Oh," he shouted back at Rod, "You've been watching movies or was your daddy in the Corps?"

"Yes, drill instructor," Rod shouted his reply as loudly as possible, "And my Grandfather, four uncles, and three cousins!"

The junior drill instructor eyed Rod for a long moment and then a small, wry smile touched the corners of his lips. .

"Then why in the hell did YOU join?" the junior DI shouted in Rod's face.

"The recruit would be disowned by the family if he joined the army, Drill Instructor!" Rod shouted back.

"Then we'll see if you can make 'em proud," he said calmly and walked away.

Joe and I surfed our way through the summer. Joe won a couple of invitationals up and down the coast.

Three months later Rod came home; a furlough to visit his family before his trip to Vietnam. He was much more muscular and leaner than he had been when he'd left home. And he had a strange look in his eye, like fear mixed with desire. We surfed and shared surf stories from the summer. While he was amazed that Joe won a few invitationals, he said he always knew it would happen one day. "I'm just surprised it happened so soon!" he exclaimed clapping Joe on the back. I could see he was genuinely happy for Joe, but there was a touch of envy behind his smile when he saw Joe's trophies.

Rod stopped over to say his good-byes before his tour of duty in Vietnam. He shook hands with Joe and me and hugged our mother. He still couldn't get Joe to join the Marines. I told him that it would be difficult to get a future World Cup champion to walk away from his sport at the peak of his career. Rod laughed. He saw my point and said that secretly he wished he'd put more into his own surfing. My mother hugged Rod once again in his khaki summer Marine uniform; a hug that was a little longer and a little tighter than usual. It was as if she was afraid to let him go. He'd been like a third son to my mother. Because Rod's mother had passed away over a year ago and had been sick for a long time before she passed, she'd been like a mother to him. Mom held his arms and looked right into Rod's eyes. She made him promise to take care of himself and stay out of harm's way.

Neither Rod nor I explained to her that because of things were heating up in Vietnam harm's way was anywhere in country. The only real safe place in the world was in the surf, on a surfboard, with the sharks, undertows, and riptides. Of course even the ocean held dangers, but they seemed minor compared to what Rod would face in Southeast Asia.

Rod left, his eyes watering, as if his parting was agony for him. We were all that there was of his family, aside from his father and he knew he might not see us again. I always wondered if at that moment Rod felt a pang of fear knowing he might not come back to his loved ones.

Being killed was the dark premonition of everyone who went to war; the clear clairvoyance of possibility in the face of deliberate and deadly violence.

During the fall Joe won several other invitationals, including one in Rocky Point, Mexico. It jetted him into the limelight as a new, up-and-coming surf star, It was also enough to qualify him for the World Cup competition and the Big Time.

The day of the World Cup competition dawned bright and blue. A strong breeze swept offshore, lifting the water then dropping it down into breaking, ten and fifteen-foot waves; a perfect day for the Surfing Association's World Cup at Doheny Beach, California. Surfers from all over the world were there—Taj Brown, Tom Carroll, and Greg Nunn among them.

Joe was in his element, the local boy with a few major invitational titles under his belt. He was the rising star everyone wanted to beat. Joe looked around for Lelani but didn't find her.

The beach at Doheny was long and full of people. Tents were set up all along the beach just out of the reach of high tide. Surfing magazines had camera crews there and a couple of helicopters floated out over the breaking surf. There was a judges' tent with a loud speaker and that was where most of the action on the beach took place.

Out on the waves several surfers sat on their boards letting the swell rise under them and then drop them into the trough. Joe was among them. He could hear the loudspeaker announce the upcoming ride by Taj Brown, the big, bronze New Zealander who already had two world cups in his trophy case. Joe watched as the sea rose up around them and Taj began to paddle with it. He felt himself lift and let it pass as Brown broke over the top and dropped down into a fair-size barrel. Joe couldn't see from where he sat but knew that Brown was carving and probably trying to turn on it.

When Brown finally came out of it, Joe smiled because he knew it was a magnificent run.

The cheering of the crowd confirmed it, but then, they generally cheered wildly for Taj, or 'The Taj,' as most people called him. He was a happy, gregarious guy whom the girls flocked around wherever he went.

Joe was next and he knew how important this tournament was. It was his first international meet and a great showing might land him a sponsor. A sponsor would allow him to step into the big time, break into the international scene, and launch a career that would take him far away from the States and Vietnam. It would be hard for the Selective Service to catch up with him in Peru, Australia, New Zealand, or Indonesia if he made it to the pro circuit.

The loudspeaker from the beach brought him back from his musings.

It was his turn.

The sea began to swell again, preparing to thrust him toward his destiny, whatever that might be. Joe began to paddle with it and as it broke over the top he jumped to his feet, stood on his board, and began to fly.

Down along the wave, he turned to carve his name along the side of the sea. Then just as the wave began to empty itself, he made a turn—one-eighty, up against the wall of water and over the top. He grabbed his board with one hand, followed by completing the turn—three-sixty, and then turned it back down and landed perfectly. Joe rode back toward the beach where the crowd went wild.

The judges gave Joe a heavy score for the three-sixty, which wasn't easy under even the best conditions.

When he stepped off his board people began slapping him on the back, shaking his hand, and one youngster shouted, "Gnarly."

Joe had to laugh.

As the crowd turned its attention back toward the surfers, Lelani stood and stared at Joe. He smiled. She was packed tightly into her white bikini, with smooth, bronze skin because she was a native Hawaiian. Her long black silk hair cascaded over her shoulders and down her back.

"Hi," she said simply. Lelani's facial expression said more than words could convey. Her eyes were filled with admiration for Joe's ride as well as love for the boy himself. "Nice ride."

Joe did not suffer from delusions of grandeur or self-importance; he just loved to surf.

"Thanks," he replied sincerely, his smile widening, as he took her in his arms and kissed her.

I always knew that surfing had been Joe's lady, but this Hawaiian girl gave him a new perspective on his relationship with the sport.

Joe looked over at the Judges' booth and saw his scores hoisted up for all to see. After the second run he was tied with the great Taj Brown.

Out in the water another surfer began to make his run. The loudspeaker announced the great Australian, Greg Nunn, who was one of Joe's personal heroes. Nunn lifted himself just as the wave broke and he dove down into the barrel and immediately tried a cutback but the wave simply ate him.

Everyone gasped and the rescue swimmers ran for the waves. Joe could see arms, then legs, then a board being jettisoned and reclaimed by the sea, almost in a heartbeat. A moment later, Nunn popped up out of the water as the wave laid itself out. He rolled onto his board and waved at the crowd to tell them that he was okay. The rescue swimmers waited for him to come in closer and then they paddled with him. Nunn looked disgusted with himself.

"Greg is one of the best there is," Lelani said with a sigh of relief, "You never know when a wave will turn on you. Bad break."

"I don't think that will stop him," Joe replied, equally relieved.

"I don't think Taj is going to stop you," she said with a wink.

Joe pondered that for a moment. After this last round, he definitely was feeling a little giddy. The best of the best was something he only knew about in other surfers like Taj Brown and Greg Nunn. If he was good, or lucky, he would join the brotherhood.

"Want to get something to drink?" Joe asked Lelani as he planted his board in the sand.

She smiled and reached out to take his hand. Joe felt the electricity jump-start though his body and they walked over to the juice stand that was set up behind the Judges' tent.

Laci and I came running down from the parking lot up above. I wasn't happy and Laci knew that the flat tire on her car that made us both late was the cause. She hoped that we didn't miss too much.

When we arrived at the Judges' tent, I scanned the standings board. It was almost as if I didn't quite recognize my own brother's name up on top ahead of Taj Brown's though tied in points. For a moment, I didn't understand.

"Joe's in first place," Laci said, "Or tied for first. That has to be good."

I turned around slowly and looked at her, as if this quick-witted, amazingly smart, incredibly beautiful, and popular girl was retarded.

"First place is okay?" I said as I almost choked, "Okay?"

Laci shrugged.

"Yeah," she replied innocently, "First place is okay, it's good."

My eyes took on the image of those of a fish as they slightly widened and seemed to bulge out.

"He's tied with Taj Brown," I sputtered, unable to believe what I was saying. "The greatest surfer in the world!"

Laci tried to let it sink in but she was too new to all this to fully understand the impact of Joe's position. Taj Brown was only a name to her. She didn't realize what a great surfer he was. She only knew she liked to watch Joe surf but hated to watch me do it because it seemed so dangerous. I assured her that it was. And I also assured her I had no intention of wiping out and getting killed.

Joe and Lelani walked up to Laci and me.

Joe smiled.

"Did you see the run?" Joe asked me.

"No, somebody took their time getting ready," I replied glancing at Laci, "But I did see the score. Man, that is gnarly!"

"It was a flat tire," Laci said, slightly embarrassed that I was blaming her for missing Joe's big moment.

Joe laughed.

"Taj Brown! Can you believe it?" Joe continued to fill me in on the events I had missed. "And Nunn took a spill.

Joe and I laughed.

"So who is your new friend?" Laci asked Joe, admiring Lelani.

"I told you about her," I said quickly.

"This is Lelani from Hawaii," Joe replied with a formal sweep of his arm, "Royal princess."

Lelani laughed.

"In the flesh," she replied, "My family is in the royal line somewhere. And I'm from Maui."

Joe and I both raised our eyebrows at the correction. Maui, of course, was in the Hawaiian Islands, but was not the same as being the island called Hawaii. Hawaii was the "Big Island" south of Maui, just close enough so that you could see it in the distance. The water around Maui was deep blue, the kind of blue that was the reason the Earth was referred to as "The Blue Planet." Tour guides on Maui told tourists that each night they went out into the water and put toilet bowl cleaner out there to keep it so blue.

Off the north shore of Maui, at the Hana State Park, the waves were monsters and the wind blew gale-force. The islanders referred to the strong winds as "stiff breezes." For surfers it was pure paradise and Joe and I both longed to go there and ride the giants. The North Shore of Oahu had been heaven.

"I told you I would come here for the World Cup," she said to Joe before turning to talk to me. "Your brother is not bad, not bad at all. The three-sixty was far out."

I beamed with pride whenever I heard something like that about my brother. I never expected such words about myself because I felt that I was not as good a surfer as Joe. Like most people who frequented the beach at Doheny, Joe was my hero.

"Are you entered in the World Cup?" Lelani asked me.

I laughed.

"Me?" I replied, "I have two problems, I'm not the surfer Joe is..."

"You'll get there," Joe interjected.

"...And second," I continued, "This one would try to kill me."

I pointed at Laci who blushed slightly.

"It looks too dangerous," Laci said with a slight smile though her eyes remained serious.

"It is," Lelani replied, "Especially with this wind blowing in offshore and kicking up the waves."

Laci's eyes widened.

"Do you surf?" she asked Lelani.

Lelani laughed.

"All Hawaiians surf," she replied, "Or at least most of them. It's in our blood. Who do you think invented surfing?"

"Seriously?" Laci was incredulous.

"And women's surfing is growing all the time," Lelani said. "Someday they'll have women surfing right along with the men in World Cup competitions like this."

Laci shook her head trying to picture herself riding a wave, carving and dropping into the barrel. She didn't even know what those terms meant but she'd heard them enough.

Off on the distant waves another surfer cross-cut a sizeable wave and tried a one-eighty; he was suddenly eaten by the water just like Nunn had been.

We all went to the juice stand, then sat down on the beach to watch the competition. Other than Taj Brown, nobody seriously challenged Joe's standing. He was certain that, in the end, it would come down to him and Brown.

As we sat down, Laci looked perplexed.

"Why do you all like surfing so much?" she asked, not quite grasping that to real surfers, surfing was not just a sport, or worse, just a recreation. It was a way of life.

Lelani looked at her like she had two heads.

"It's a spiritual thing," I replied, recalling what Joe and all the other surfers had told me over the years.

Laci continued to look puzzled, even scowled a little. It wasn't the answer she was expecting. I supposed she expected me to say something like it was fun, but I was capable of higher meaning being on the Principal's Honor Roll.

"A spiritual thing?" she asked, her tone skeptical.

"We came from the sea," Joe replied, beginning the litany of surfing cosmology, "Like the earth, we are mostly water, in fact, salt water runs in our veins. When we ride the waves, we commune with the ocean and the earth."

Laci thought for a moment and then her eyes suddenly brightened.

"It's kind of like God?" she replied, her own epiphany unfolding before our eyes. Laci was Catholic, like Joe and I. However, I only went to church a few times, mostly for funerals and weddings. I didn't know much about church stuff except what I learned at Saint Monica's.

"What, the ocean?" Lelani asked.

Laci nodded more enthusiastically. "The ocean is so big and we're so small," she replied, "Kind of like how we are with God who created everything."

We all thought for a moment and then nodded. If God created everything, including the oceans and the monsters off the North Shore and Waimea, then he had to be really, really big. Just like the oceans could give us a cool ride or crush us like a bug, God had the same kind of power only over everything there was, including the ocean.

Laci continued, "The only thing is, God is a like a person and we can have a personal relationship with Him."

We all smiled at that. Laci didn't understand that we all had a personal relationship with the sea. The sea could make us smile or make us cry; she could even kill us as a few of the world's best surfers who were cut down in their prime, evidenced.

"And the surf board," Laci continued, "That brings you in contact with the sea; kind of in-between like Jesus does with God, the Father."

There was something original—surfing theology. But in a way she was right although none of us had ever thought about it like that; Jesus as a surf board, a stick, ripping through the waves of our lives. With his hair and beard, I could imagine Jesus as a surfer, riding the waves at Galilee.

Cool.

We talked more about surfing and spirituality as we watched the competition. Joe and I got into an argument over who was the greatest surfer in the world.

"Got to be Laird Humble," Joe said definitively, "Best big wave surfer, best all around."

"No, Gerry Velasquez," I replied, "Why do you think they call him, 'Mr. Pipeline'?"

"Laird has been riding since he was seven years old," Joe replied firmly, as if that would end the argument once and for all.

But even though I didn't surf as well as my older brother, I knew just as much about surfing history and the surfing scene. We read all the same magazines and talked to all the same surfers. I was entitled to my opinions as well.

"So?" I replied as the two girls smiled at each other, "Lopez is older and has been surfing longer!"

The girls looked at each other as if they'd just discovered the inside track into the world of surfing guys. It was, as they suspected, like two kids in the sand box arguing over which GI Joe was better, the Astronaut or the Marine.

I liked the Astronaut.

"It might not be either of them," Lelani said loudly enough for everyone to hear and to get our attention. She looked directly at Joe, "It could be you."

This stopped the argument. Joe could become the greatest surfer in the world, I thought with distinct pride. In fact he might already have earned that honor.

Joe reached down and fingered some grains of sand.

"Why do we do this?" he asked as if questioning it for the first time.

The silence temporarily engulfed us amid the background din of the competition. It was a very big question that I thought we had answered; but I realized that it was even bigger than we first suspected.

I thought hard.

"Because we have to," I replied quietly as Joe and Lelani looked at me intently. It was one of those moments when the Principal's Honor Roll took over in my brain and pushed me toward philosophy. It was real and palatable and had meaning.

"Like you said," I continued, looking at Joe, "We come from the sea and have salt water in our blood."

And that was that.

It was Joe's second run, and the waves were running higher as the Sun began its own run toward the sea.

I watched closely as his turn came. The water swelled and he caught it jumping to his feet immediately. He carved and crosscut, turning so that he could start his one-eighty. As he started up, inexplicably, the wave simply ate him and all I could see was his stick pop out of the white water. He was okay but a little downhearted as he recovered his board and rode the rest of the wave in.

But it was all right because Taj still had to make his run and the waves were growing restless.

Taj Brown made his run and it was flawless despite the fast, heavy waves. Joe fell a few points behind.

"The wave just took me, Man," Joe said as he lumbered up with his board on his head. He stuck it into the ground and I handed him a towel.

"It's getting rough out there," he said as he shook his head and watched another surfer wipe out.

Lelani put her arm around his shoulder.

"You know, in Maui, we say that the sea is a jealous woman," she said, "If you think about something else while you're with her, she'll swat you."

Joe eyed Lelani for a long minute and I knew he was thinking to himself that if there was anything else he was thinking about out there, it was her. Still, he thought that he should make the perfect ride anyway.

"You are thinking about me," Lelani said plainly, "Let's be real here. Don't worry about it and just get back to the wave."

Joe smiled. He never met anyone like Lelani who would speak straight out instead of hiding and masking what she had to say.

He nodded and she returned his smile.

"You win this and we'll see a lot more of each other," she said, "I follow the World Cup series everywhere."

Finally, Joe's name was called and he paddled out to take his place in the lineup.

Greg Nunn made a great run ahead of Joe and moved up in the standing to tie with him. But Joe didn't worry. He had his final run coming and even though the sea was still rough with spray flying everywhere off the white water, he felt that he was going to do it this time. He thought about what Laci said about the surfboard and the sea and how it was like Jesus and God. He'd learned all about that when he went to Saint Monica Catholic. While we were both baptized Catholic, we never did a lot of going to Mass. But if Joe was being called by anything, he was being called by the sea and the surf.

He turned and felt the ocean swell. Immediately he lay down on the board and began to paddle. His board felt good underneath him, solid, like it was meant to be there. Jesus. What a rush.

He felt the wave catch and he jumped to his feet dropping down over the curl onto the front of the wave. He turned, carved, crosscut and shot up over the top of the wave, then grabbed his board with his hand. He turned a perfect three-sixty and flipped a somersault landing perfectly in front of the forming barrel. He crouched and let his trailing hand drag along in the water behind him. The barrel began to close and he turned downward, increasing his speed and emerging just before the wave collapsed.

He could hear the crowd going wild once again.

And he smiled. Jesus.

On the beach, as Lelani, Laci, I, and about a thousand others raced up to Joe, the judges came down with another heavy score. They'd never seen two 360s done at once along two different axis. Neither had I.

We were suddenly flooded by fans.

Joe was all smiles, shaking hands and hugging girls all the while keeping an eye on Lelani for her reaction. Just as suddenly as it all started, everyone around us went quiet and turned to watch the next surfer, Taj Brown, make his run. With a near perfect ride, Taj would top Joe and win his third World Cup.

Taj began to paddle as the wave swelled underneath him. He caught it, stood and dropped down the face to carve and crosscut. As he turned upwards on the face, he shot up back over top the curl, executed a beautiful three-sixty with a side twist, and then headed back down. He landed perfectly, but the capricious white water suddenly obliterated him.

"I know how it feels," Joe said as the crowd groaned and then turned to cheer the heir-apparent to the World Cup.

Lelani screamed and jumped on Joe while Laci looked questioningly excited. I couldn't quite fathom what just happened. My brother, Joe Connors, was suddenly the local boy made good.

Joe won by several points and Taj Brown was gracious with his congratulations as he came ashore. The judges presented Joe with a massive World Cup from the International Surfing Association and Joe was a champion. World Champion.

The interviews and photographs took what seemed like hours. Joe handed out so many autographs, on magazines, paper, surfboards, and even a few bikini tops. Several sponsors gathered around to offer their proposals and it looked as if Joe was on his way. The new tour started in three weeks down in Australia. Laci was excited without really knowing why. I told her that Joe was now a champion, a World Champion and her eyes went wide. She suddenly jumped on me and kissed me squarely on the lips!

"What was that for?" I asked as she slipped back down onto the sand, "I'm not the world champion."

Laci blushed and waved her hand around.

"You know, with all the excitement," she replied and then looked demurely at the sand, "because I wanted to."

I smiled.

"I liked it," I said gently, and I reached down to kiss her back. The second one was much better, deep, intimate, intense, bells ringing, choirs of angels. When I finally released her, she wavered a bit as if drunk, blinked, and then regained her composure.

We couldn't say any more than that, so we rejoined the celebration for the World Champion, Joe Connors of Pacific Palisades, California. My brother.

Joe chose Billabong as a sponsor because they paid him immediately—$10,000—and moved him directly into the pro circuit. Boxes of surfing equipment arrived at the house, all prominently displaying the Billabong logo. Four long boards and six short boards also arrived and Joe gave me one of each. There were beachcombers, t-shirts, polo shirts, and a couple of blue and yellow wet suits with short and long bottoms for cold and warm water surfing. So many leashes arrived that Joe had to give them away at the beach, which was probably the point.

There was deep perfection in Lelani, something Joe called symmetry. She was the perfect young woman.

That first night after everyone went home, they lay in the sand as the sun sank blithely into the sea. The shore patrol drove by and waved. Because it was Joe, the new world champion, the park was his, even after closing.

Joe kissed Lelani lightly on the lips. She was his surfer girl now and she responded with deepening passion. In a few moments, her bikini—both top and bottoms—lay next to them on the sand. The rising moon glistened off her skin. Joe's hands were gentle and artistic, the way he'd become at surf riding. He saw the swell of her breasts in the rising moonlight, her nipples forming perfect peaks. He began his approach toward the lip. As the barrel opened, he dropped down and entered, meeting the Mother Earth where she was. When the wave exploded, he fell into the bronze water and became one with his wahini, a world champion with a princess from the Royal Hawaiian Family. He was favored and destined for great things.

Joe and Lelani returned to our house in the early morning and then went immediately to his room.

When my mother got up for work, she checked on us. I asleep like the little angel I hadn't been for years, and Joe together with Lelani.

She stood for a while in the doorway watching the two of them sleep. She smiled at her son and what she hoped was her future daughter-in-law.

I wondered if I could get away with the same thing. Of course, Laci and I were under-age and then there was the little matter of her parents.

Lelani stayed at our house for the week before Joe was to start the tour, with my mother's blessing. Actually, my mother liked having another girl in the house, kind of like a daughter or a little sister. Lelani seemed happy to do girl-things.

Chapter Six

The following week, Joe and Lelani took off for the pro circuit tour. They would go to Australia, New Zealand, Indonesia, the Solomon Islands, and Fiji. After that they would swing back toward Hawaii, Peru, Mexico, and the California coast. They'd hit all the hot surfing beaches; Huntington Beach, Malibu, Doheny, and the Mavericks up in Half Moon Bay near San Francisco. The Mavericks was a recent discovery in the cold water off the northern coast. It was reported to have waves as big and dangerous as at Waimea. In other words, it was a full-scale monster.

Without Joe or Rod around, Laci and I began to see more of each other outside of school. We went to the beach a lot, did a couple of picnics, went to the movies, hung around at each other's homes. I tried to keep her away from my mother who craved female companionship and would divert Laci's full attention away from me.

While Joe was in Australia, he called home.

Laci and I went to the beach so that she might grieve again at my surfing and I might get her into the water to actually teach her the joys of surfing.

We arrived at Malibu in the early afternoon. Of course it was still winter, but winter on the beach at Malibu only meant that the water was a little cooler and the waves were a little more promising. I took the precaution of bringing my smallest wetsuit in anticipation of her possible objection to the water temperature. She made that objection, and when I reached into my bag to pull out the wetsuit, she scowled. I told her that surfing was more fun than a basket toss. The basket toss was a cheerleading move where several cheerleaders toss one of their squad into the air, the airborne cheerleader spins and lands on her back in the arms of the other cheerleaders. This piqued her interest. What finally convinced her was when I told her that we would only go on the little waves, those that would actually hit the beach; and that way she would spend more time with me. I got my opportunity to show Laci why I loved surfing.

She looked really good in the skin-tight wetsuit, really even better than I ever dreamed. I shifted away from the distraction of a girl in a wetsuit to the problem at hand. I told her that we would only ride the surfboards on our stomachs and she seemed happy with that. Laci was very athletic, so I was certain that it wouldn't take her long to learn how to move the board. Soon she would learn how to stand up and balance on it.

We paddled out, cresting the first and second set of waves where we sat on our boards and waited. I explained about catching the wave and then riding it along the face to try to stay out of the white water where even a little wave could gobble you up.

As the wave began to swell under us, I looked at her and saw her eyes widen.

"Lay down on the board and start paddling toward the shore," I shouted with a smile.

She did and caught the wave the very first time. I leaned away from the white water.

"Lean like me!" I shouted as we started down the short front of the wave.

She did and slid down easily away as the wave continued over the top amid its gentle roar.

I saw her smile and knew I had her hooked. She even laughed as the wave played out and deposited us near the shore.

"Let's do it again," she said, her smile growing even larger. Nobody ever stayed on the board the first time, but she did.

We did do it again, and again, and again. She even tried to stand a couple of times but wound up in the sea.

"It's so cool," she said as she walked up onto the shore after retrieving her board, "Underneath the waves, it's so cool. They look like tubes spreading out and everything underneath is calm."

We sat and drank some soda while we watched the other beginners out on the gentle waves. I then showed her how to jump up on her board without dragging her knee, which, of course, threw her off balance and tossed her into the ocean.

We paddled out again and caught another wave. We paddled with it until I shouted, "Jump!"

Both of us jumped up on our boards at the same moment.

"Bend your knees, extend your arms," I shouted, showing her the stance.

She mimicked me and rode the wave down but lost her balance and wound up in the ocean again. But Laci was absolutely tenacious, paddling out again and again.

Finally, she rode a wave the whole way in and stepped off her board. She laughed and jumped around like a crazy person. Now she was officially a surfer girl.

We sat on the blanket as the sun began its final run into the west. Laci was famished and quickly ate two of the sandwiches that she made. I told her that I'd help out of her wetsuit if she liked and she agreed.

She unzipped the top and pulled it back onto her arms. I could not help but gulp mightily at the sight at the thought of removing clothing even though this was more like removing a jacket. I helped her pull her arms out of the suit and then shook it to remove the excess water. She pulled the wetsuit pants off and nearly dragged her bikini bottom with it. I suddenly grew giddy, my teenage-boy hormones running amok. I stared for a long moment and then turned to watch the other surfers again.

As I sat there watching them, I tried as much as I could to think about their techniques and their styles. It's what other surfers did. Suddenly, I felt Laci's hand on my shoulder and when I turned, before I could shift into "cool," she kissed me gently on the lips. Coolness never even had a chance and I felt like a child in the midst of a wondrous new experience. I lifted my hands to her face as if it were the most natural thing to do and slowly caressed the soft sides of her strong but slender neck. Her breathing grew more rapid and shallow as I glided my hand across her shoulder, accidentally knocking the strap of her bikini top off. She gasped and I pulled my hand away as if I had just touched a hot burner.

"Why did you stop?" she rasped, her breathing growing even shallower and rapid until I thought she might hyperventilate. Clearly Laci was made for this kind of thing.

"I-I thought I did something wrong," I sputtered knowing full well that I was way out of my league in experience. Laci, on the other hand, I was certain, was experienced at this sort of thing, though I didn't know why I thought that.

We both turned to watch the remaining surfers come in as the golden, fiery disk of the Sun dipped slowly, and was cooled by the emerald green sea.

Soon, as Laci recovered her composure, we were alone though I knew it wouldn't be long before the beach patrol would run us off.

"Didn't you want me to stop?" I asked finally, staring into her large, gray eyes. I saw longing in them.

Longing? I suddenly needed to get back onto my surfboard but before I could move, Laci dropped the other strap of her bikini top.

All that remained was for me to reach. My hand trembled as I extended it and she leaned closer, perfectly willing. Just as my fingers grabbed the flimsy material, the beach patrol pulled up.

"Beach is closed, kids," the megaphone blared.

*

Oceans away, Joe walked in out of the surf with his long board. He'd just come off a fifteen-foot curl swinging into the barrel and then out before the whole thing collapsed. Lelani was all smiles when she handed him a towel.

"You scored good on that one, Mate!" Lelani said in her attempt at an Australian accent. She had been working on it for the last month.

Joe laughed as he put his arm around her.

He was leading the Billabong Pro Grom out at Orewa beach and loving it. After three rides, he had a six-point lead over Taj Brown. He and the Taj had become good friends. They enjoyed showing off for each other and trying to out-do the one another and a couple of times they forgot they were in a World Cup competition. Taj had wiped-out completely in front of Joe and they slapped hands as Joe paddled out. Taj was all smiles anyway because he did a three-sixty with a waggling somersault before he wiped out. He knew this would set Joe off. Joe was also learning to love Lelani who was patient and thoroughly interested in his surfing. She surfed well herself but didn't enter any of the fledgling women's tournaments. Joe observed that women surfers were lighter on the boards and could maneuver like crazy. He never saw any male surfer get so far back into a tube and then escape before it collapsed. He had never been able to do that himself. He pictured women challenging male surfers straight up one day, beauty against brawn. Lelani was graceful on the waves, flying like a bird in full glide upon the wind.

Off the northern coast of New Zealand the wind was kicking up, being pushed by a typhoon two hundred miles out. If they didn't finish up tomorrow, then they'd have to postpone the final event and run for the hills. Joe always wanted to ride the really big waves fueled by a super storm. He'd heard of sixty-foot waves, twice the size of those at Mavericks and Waimea. Secretly, he figured it was a death wish that all surfers had to go down, swallowed by a monster instead of growing old and dying in your sleep on land somewhere.

*

I stopped by the mailbox as I arrived home from school. The weather was heavily overcast and rainy and the waves were running good off Doheny. In the mail there were the typical bills—electric, telephone—a flyer for a local hardware store and a letter that caught my eye; it was addressed to Joe and the return address read: "Selective Service Administration." Immediately, I knew what it was. Joe was headed for Indonesia. If the military wanted him, they weren't going to get him. I decided right then that I wouldn't tell my mother because she would only worry and try to contact Joe. And I knew full well that he wouldn't come home just to enter the Army. He was a surfer and out on the waves was where he was supposed to be. Besides, if he never heard about the notice, or saw it, he couldn't be held responsible. If they ever came to arrest him once he got back, he could always say—truthfully—that he never received it.

I couldn't escape the thought, however, that this would end badly. You didn't mess with Uncle Sam.

Still, I put the letter under my mattress. The next day, I awoke to the sound of tapping on my window. Groggily, I slipped out of bed and pulled back the curtain. It was Laci. As I opened the window and Laci began to climb inside, her eyes suddenly widened and she smiled hugely. It took me a moment but I realized that I was still dressed as I slept, that is, not dressed at all!

I grabbed at my sheet, tried to wrap it around me and fell flat onto my face. With my naked backside sticking up in the air, I wanted to die.

"You don't have to be embarrassed," Laci whispered, "I think you're beautiful."

Quickly, I covered myself and turned over to sit on the floor. My mind raced.

As I gazed at Laci, she suddenly began to lower both straps of her bikini top. Slowly, she let them fall. Her breasts were small but proportionate to her slim form. They were perfectly round with exquisitely sculptured nipples. She was beautiful beyond reason. I was glad, at that moment, that I had covered myself with the sheet. It became a tense moment and only my confusion and lack of knowledge kept us from missing surfing that day.

"It's only fair," she whispered.

According to my teenage hormones, I was in love even though I didn't yet know what love was. If I had only been brighter, more perceptive, I would have known that she was most assuredly in love with me. She had plans, ambitions for her future. She wanted to get away from her parents. Although she loved them, they had spent the last eight years of her life pushing her into a music career, preventing her from enjoying her childhood. They isolated her from others her age, boys especially, and told everyone who would listen that one day she would become a star. Her life was like a cocoon and her playing with me was one way of rebelling, grasping at something outside of it. In the process, she had fallen in love like a regular teenage girl.

I put my head down on my knees and tried to breathe. My friends always talked about this, some bragged about it because that's what teenage boys did. I laughed along with them, shared the crude joke, and made comments about girls and what I wanted to do with them.

But nothing I ever did or said prepared me for this. Here I was with a half-naked beauty, I was totally naked except for a sheet, and my mother had gone to work for the whole day

It would have been every young man's dream if Laci wasn't the most perfect girl ever. Who could think of manhandling the Venus di Milo? Certainly I couldn't!

Laci stared at me as the sunlight flooded in around her slender body, accenting and highlighting her skin and the curves of her breasts and hips.

My mind began to scream at me to move, embrace my manhood by embracing Laci, but my body wouldn't respond.

Laci seemed to understand more than I did and she smiled and slowly lifted her top back up to cover herself. Securing her straps, she stepped over to me, knelt, and leaned to kiss me lightly on my lips.

"I'll wait outside," she whispered. And she climbed back out the window.

Had I been just a year older, I probably would have died of a heart attack.

*

The sky was a dismal blue, a flat, innocuous blue that didn't seem to offer much hope as it crowned a sea of wavering, pending green. The sun hovered, like a ravenous predator in the hot, humid air. You needed a life jacket in order to not drown where you stood.

Rod sat on the bench with two of his new squad-mates. The Huey helicopter rattled at just two-hundred feet nearly brushing the canopy below. A door gunner stood vigilant, his hand resting on the trigger guard of the M213 .50 caliber machine gun mounted just below and outside the door. He scanned the jungle below, waiting for a sign. There was never a time to let up in this business because there was no R & R in the sky. Charlie, the Viet Cong, always looked up, waiting for air superiority to touch down, then it was his game and he knew it.

Rod and his two squad-mates were headed for a fire-base out in the middle of the Iron Triangle; a makeshift quasi-fortress of sandbags, plywood, and foo gas on the perimeter to welcome Charlie during his nightly visits.

FNGs, fucking new guys, is what the three squad-mates were called. They were fresh meat, completely expendable and not out in the jungle long enough to survive and earn the respect of a "living" Marine.

The chopper landed in an open space, a landing zone or LZ that was located next to the slightly elevated fire-base. The LZ was created by C4 high explosive and foo gas burning away the foliage.

Rod surveyed the scene and realized that he was a long way from Malibu and Doheny. It was a long way from any ocean, any surf, and any barrel except the barrel of a gun. The Green Room was different here, a deadly green where shadows often unloaded with an AK-47 on full auto.

Rod began to think about Joe and the choices the two of them had made, together, and now separately—Joe, a surfer of the sea, and Rod, a soldier of the jungle.

As the chopper settled into the returning grass, Rod heard shots fired and felt something whiz past him. There were loud clanking sounds where holes began to appear in the bulkhead near him; that something caught one of his fellow replacements and knocked him out of the helicopter.

"Get out, get out!" the door gunner screamed as he opened up with the M213 at the nearby jungle. Rod and his remaining squad-mate jumped out, landing and stumbling over the body of their newly-fallen comrade who did not actually log a second on the ground at the fire-base.

No time for heroics. Easy come, easy go.

*

Joe cut a one-eighty and carved down off the lip. He turned again and shot back up. For four heavenly seconds he rode the lip racking up points.

Indonesia was awesome. He had surfed Razors, Keramas, and Lacerations off East Bali. Off Lombok, he took on Senggigi and Desert Point. Off Mentawai, he did Botik Island, Lance's Left and Kandui Left. But now, he was tearing up Indicators and the Uluwatu Pro Grom. This was the final heat and he knew he'd score a perfect ten. Taj Brown came up short dropping his last wave.

New World Champ.

Lelani jumped up and down excitedly as Joe rode into the beach. The crowd cheered,

When the judges posted, the crowd cheered again. It was official, another win for Joe Connors.

"You're still the king!" Lelani shouted as she jumped into Joe's arms and wrapped her legs around him. She locked her lips over his.

Surfers were notoriously free-spirited. It's one thing Joe liked about the lifestyle. All of the guys had girls, usually two or more at any one time. Girls hit on Joe all the time but one look at Lelani always set him straight. Whenever she came onto the beach, Joe could see all the others pause and gaze. He could feel the longing because Lelani was like a superstar. She walked with grace and ease, her long, silky, black hair streaming in the sea breeze, often dancing around her face. And she surfed like she was born to it, which, of course, she was,

"Did you see that lip?" Joe asked, excited like a kid.

Lelani laughed and nodded, turning the edge of her hand into a surfboard riding the top of the world.

Chapter Seven

Rod fell heavily against a wall near the bridge that crossed the Phu Cam Canal. He and the rest of Company A, First Battalion, First Marines, had barely arrived from Phu Bai, which was eight miles south of the city. Phu Bai was the headquarters of Task Force X-Ray, which meant it was also the forward HQ for the First Marine Division in South Vietnam. Reports from inside Hue City suggested that some NVA and Viet Cong had infiltrated and attacked government positions including the MACV compound located south of the Perfume River and the ARVN compound located in the Citadel north of the River. The Citadel was the older part of the city built by some 19th Century emperor before the French waltzed in and took it all over. Because attacks had broken out in all parts of the country at the same time, the information from Hue was confused and sketchy at best.

Rod and every other Marine in A/1/1, however, knew that it wasn't just "some" NVA and VC that were wreaking havoc in Hue but several battalions and possibly a whole division. Bullets had rained in from all directions the entire four hours they'd been there. The barrage was so thick the shots were like 7.62X39mm gnats buzzing around everyone's heads. Two of Rod's buddies lay face down in the street, bitten by those gnats.

One of the M48 tanks they'd met and followed into the city sat smoldering nearby, victim of a fusillade of recoilless rifle fire that swarmed in on it and tore it apart.

Rod followed GSgt. Walt Norton into a building as plaster from the walls exploded all around them. Glass came from somewhere and flew like a thousand tiny blades tearing at their skin and their fatigues.

The machine gun that they were after suddenly erupted from the top of the stairs inside and nearly caught Norton. But he was ready as he came in and slipped around the corner untouched. Rod raised his M-14 and sprayed the upstairs catching one of the enemy soldiers as the others slipped upstairs.

"Damn it!" Norton shouted as he spun from around the corner and started up the set of steps. Rod covered him as he cautiously followed. Suddenly, an explosion rocked the upstairs and Norton flew back down where Rod caught him.

It could have been a mortar round from another NVA position across the street, a grenade from anybody, or even a tank round from the other M48 still trying to take out the machine gun. Entering buildings to clear them meant that you were suddenly high on everyone's target list because no one could identify you.

Two more explosions sent Rod and GSgt. Norton tumbling into the street back the way they'd entered. They ran for the wall where another machine gun from across the canal opened up on them.

"Are you fucking kidding me?" Norton snarled.

The Marines were desperately trying to get to the MACV compound where elements of the U.S. Army's First Calvary and other Marines had already been attacked by the NVA and VC. They had used machine guns and B-40 rockets but hesitated in their all-out assault. That was just long enough for the Marines to get their act together. Still, several guys had already bought it.

Rod peered out at the water of the canal, dancing with the wind, the occasional exploding round, and the rain that just started to fall. It was the first time in a month that he'd had a moment to reconsider his decision to join. Maybe surfing with Joe the rest of his days would have been better, given him more days. He didn't think he, or anyone else in A/1/1, had much of a chance of surviving.

Suddenly, inexplicably, Norton jumped up and charged across the bridge with his rifle blazing on full automatic. He dove behind a wall, and launched a grenade into the machine gun nest that was pinning his men down. Rod had never seen anything like it! It was like Sgt. Dan Daley at Belleau Wood or "Manila" John Basilone of Guadalcanal, charging directly into the jaws of the enemy.

"Move it!" Norton shouted, and Rod and the others jumped from their positions charging onto the bridge.

None of them knew it, but it would be a long three weeks in Hue.

*

Joe sat by himself on the beach. The sun hung low near the lip of the world in the west. The seas were relatively calm, short right break with the wind blowing east to southeast.

He was sitting just east of Lunga Point on Guadalcanal in the Solomon Islands. One of the other surfers in Honiara mentioned something about Vietnam and the terrible fighting that suddenly broke out all over the country on their biggest holiday. It was like attacking someone on Christmas.

Joe looked down at the copy of Surfer magazine that someone gave him. It showed Joe out on a wave off the coast of Australia with the title, "World Champion, 1967." He thought about the others, the ones who were sensational and challenged him at every meet; guys like Corky Carroll, Mickey Munoz and the Hoffman brothers, Walt and Phil. They were the ones that kept him on the edge and helped him forget about 'Nam and Rod. But someone brought it up, so he borrowed a jeep and drove out by himself to think.

Joe looked around slowly, up and down the coastline, with its wide beaches and the jungle beyond. There were a few surfers out on the waves, some kids playing in the sand. Lelani was still back at the hotel in Honiara. As he watched the surfers ride the small waves, he thought about Rod for the first time since he started the tour. He pictured him in a battle and wondered who was watching his back.

It didn't take Joe long to make the connection. There was Rod, in the Marines, fighting a battle in Vietnam, and here he sat on the beach, near the infamous Red Beach where Marines stormed ashore twenty-six years earlier. Fighting instead of surfing, everywhere around the world, Joe couldn't get it to add up. It was a deadly thing to face an enemy bullet but also a dead-as-a-door-nail thing to face thirty foot waves off the North Shore on Oahu at the Pipeline. Either way a person could wind up very dead.

He would surf tomorrow off Maravagi, just north of the Canal. The motor launch would take him and the other surfers in the Solomon Invitational across Iron Bottom Sound where the hulks of American and Japanese warships rested after a great naval battle. This place was fraught with history and it weighed on Joe.

He thought about Rod again and gazed out at the water.

In the distance, a wave began to swell, larger than the ones today. The tide was rising. When it hit the surfers, they were not ready and they all wiped out. From there, it drove toward the beach and the children screamed gleefully and ran toward the jungle. The water ran up onto the shore and around Joe's feet and legs. He dipped his hand into it.

"Starstuff," he thought," it's all related, from this salt water and this beach, to the jungles of Vietnam and the stars and galaxies far, far away."

At Maravagi, Joe surfed more seriously than he normally did, Something was driving him and the others noticed, especially Lelani.

Joe used one of Hobie's newer, short boards, supposed to be more maneuverable and aerobatic. In the final round, trailing Carroll by two points, he caught a nice twelve foot wave and shot down the front, turning at the bottom and riding across up toward the lip. He caught it, ripped a one-eighty and then dropped down onto a false chop he couldn't see and wiped out completely.

Lelani sighed.

It wasn't all surfing and fun. Racial tensions and tensions from the war in Vietnam increased all around the country. At our high school, boys that we knew who were older than us and had gone off to war began arriving home in pieces if they arrived home at all.

The first was Sharon Harrington's brother, John. We were in Spanish class, trying to get our Español to rock-and-roll when the word came in over the PA system. The principal told us of the tragedy, how the alumnus of our school had gone to Vietnam to do his duty. I knew John., His sister who sat two rows in front of me in Mrs. Whoever's Spanish class. John didn't know jack about duty. He had simply been given a M213 door machine gun on the door of a Bell 1-UHD Iroquois Helicopter and been taught to shoot it. He'd taken a round above the breastplate and had fallen out of the chopper.

He was dead, very dead, extensively dead, terminally dead. Apparently someone had forgotten to tell Sharon.

Silencío, there was complete silence in the classroom. The Spanish teacher reacted quickly ordering a couple of the other girls to take Sharon to the nurse's office, give her an aspirin. Semper Fi.

Laci was a bit confused at my stunned silence. I knew about Vietnam, did a report about the lush, green, verdant country. It seemed like a good place to fight over, rockets' red glare and home of the bereaved.

I went home that night and pulled out the yearbook from the previous school year. All the photographs of seniors were in Kodachrome Technicolor. None of the seniors would ever look that good again, especially John.

My photographs had always been in black and white and often my name was spelled wrong. But this year mine was in color too, a Kodachrome rite of passage.

I wondered how I should handle John's photo: mark a big "X" through it, one down, fifty-two thousand more to go.

It was 1968 and it didn't end there.

Another student, two years ahead of us and one of the surfers came back from Vietnam. He showed up at school in his Marine dress blues, a poster boy for the Marine Corps; but you couldn't shake his hand, either hand. Protruding from his sleeves were two prosthetic hooks. His name was Woody and his surfing days were probably over; it was hard to handle a board with hooks.

I was one of the few guys who took Home Economics. I wanted to be a well-rounded person and wanted to learn how to flip pancakes, make pizza, bake chocolate chip cookies, and darn a hole in my socks. One of the girls in the class, Connie, was there immersed in tears, wet beyond all reason. She was one of the tough, though beautiful girls, one of the strong ones, who could dish out anything and take anything, but that day she was sobbing.

The tears were foreign to me, especially coming from someone like Connie; I didn't know what to do. I reached out, put my hand on her shoulder and asked her what was wrong.

She gave a one word answer, Gary.

Gary. I knew she had a boyfriend by that name. He was one of those tough guys who enlisted in the army and went to Vietnam.

I thought he must be dead—he must have died for his country like so many of the other guys from our school.

"No," she replied, "He didn't die for his country; he was maimed for his country."

Connie's boyfriend had stepped on a land mine and lost both his legs. He would get no color guard, no eulogy, no flag-draped coffin processing on a caisson to his final resting place. For Gary, there would be no walking across a stage to receive a college degree, no escorting his bride down the aisle on their wedding day, no first dance when his daughter got married. There was only a Purple Heart and a soul full of grief.

Everything happened so fast that March of 1968.

There was still more: John Chandler was captain of the football team and a great surfer, as well as captain of the surf team. Even Joe admired him. In March of 1968, the Ides of March, he led his Marine squad into the elephant grass and was run over by a .50 caliber lawn mower. He alone survived but would never play football again. Or surf for that matter. I could see it in his eyes when he showed up at school in a wheelchair to visit the old gang. They were distant with that thousand-yard stare.

Most of the old gang had gone on to new gangs: 3rd Marines, 101st Airborne, the Big Red One, 1st infantry division of the United States Army. The only surfing these boys did was in the rice patties of Vietnam. And there was no beach break or applause at the end of the ride.

It became hard for me to surf sometimes. I would sit on my board and wait for the swell. I would look at the horizon and just knew that "over there" was coming closer and closer to Joe—and maybe even closer to me.

Surfing in a world at war with itself was problematic. Surfing embraced a positive vision and the natural power of the sea, while war only embraced death and destruction.

Out there, on the waves, they were bound to meet; it was destiny.

I was hard pressed to understand why Laci seemed so oblivious to what was happening in the world. The week had been hellish, the red of the stripes on the flag seemed to run and bleed into the white. And the week that Sousa died, my mind was distracted by the meat grinder called Vietnam, 'Nam, or simply, "The Shit."

My poetry dropped off and what did up show-up took on an ominous tone and Laci would tend to her studies instead of talking when we are alone before school at the lunch tables. Sometimes, Laci seems to live in our own little world while the shroud of foreboding seemed to pass over mine.

It wasn't the best of times.

*

Meanwhile, a boat took Joe, Lelani, and the other surfers out to Cloudbreak, an isolated reef five miles off the shores of Fiji. And Joe rode the surf, and he flew, and he continued his winning ways.

How far was Cloudbreak from the Ashau Valley? More than mere miles, more than a whole planet; it was a different reality, a place where culture was old, set like an eternal timepiece that sung out the seconds that rang in whole generations.

Wave riders, all of them.

Chapter Eight

Spring Break of that year was special. Joe and Lelani returned from the Tour and Rod returned, in one piece, from Vietnam.

They all returned to a changed America. The summer of love was transforming, a final breaking of the zeitgeist; the crumbling of imperial America. The *status quo* was in disarray, its institutions trembled, and the Old Guard languished.

Rod was much grimmer than he was before he went overseas and the joy of life seemed to have been drained from him. His summer of love hadn't involved hippies or full blown barrels forming out of tangents and the increasing energy in rising swells. His had come from the barrel of a .308 M-16 automatic rifle.

Rod did go out with us to surf off Malibu, but he fell and didn't bother to get back up. I retrieved his board. He walked up onto the beach and sat on the sand, watching silently.

Joe and Lelani both tried to get him back into the water.

"Come on, Bro," Joe called out, "It's like riding a bike!"

"Thanks, man, I know," Rod replied and then went silent.

Rod had been promoted to gunnery sergeant and had, unbelievably, signed up for another tour of duty in Vietnam.

Joe was stunned. He thought Rod would finish his enlistment at Camp Pendleton in Oceanside near San Diego and the two of them could surf Trestles together.

When Joe asked him why, Rod replied that the work wasn't done.

Joe had a hard time understanding Rod and his slide into the bad vibe. Was the war such a complete downer that it would change a dude like Rod? Looking around he could see that the whole country was going over the falls.

Lelani said that this war wasn't really about ridding the world of tyranny, what could a little country like Vietnam do to the world?

It was politics, paranoia, and maybe greed that fueled it. The people in this country began to recognize this and they realized it wasn't what America was about.

We made it through the holidays. I went to Easter Mass with Laci and her family. It was the first time that I'd been in a church since my dad left us. It never seemed like there was much point. After all, God didn't prevent my mother's heart break.

I must have aged a bit, maybe gained a little wisdom out there on the waves. I knew I had to think about more than just myself, Joe, and my mother. Rod was going off to war *again*, and he could die. Many of the boys from my high school had already been wounded or killed. Then there was the whole country, people like myself and my mother who were going crazy over events in the world. Maybe it was time to set aside my anger and learn how to pray.

I really didn't know what it was all about, but it didn't seem to concern Laci any. She seemed happy, healthy, and wise.

In April of 1968, the fabric of society began to pull apart in earnest.

On April 4, the great Dr. Martin Luther King, Jr. was assassinated in Memphis; shot down just outside his hotel room. King was truly the moral leader of the country, taking on the civil rights issue during the years just after the Civil Rights Act of 1964 had been passed.

King understood that no law could, in and of itself, restore natural rights to a socially enslaved people suddenly freed.

He knew that only the changing human heart could deliver justice.

King never wanted anything but equal rights and opportunities. He didn't want extra action, affirmative or otherwise. He didn't want racial quotas or multiculturalism with its inherent exclusivity. He loved all humankind.

Like he said in his famous, 'I Have a Dream Speech:' "I have a dream that my four little children will one day live in a nation where they will not be judged by the color of their skin but by the content of their character."

Martin Luther King, Jr. was a gnarly dude.

The shock of the brutal slaying swiftly turned to anger. Fueled by the Black Panthers, a Black radical group, riots broke out in many major cities. The Watts section of Los Angeles, a predominantly black part of the city, was set on fire.

I never could understand why people would destroy their own homes and businesses. Were they going to move everyone to Beverly Hills?

We were told to stay out of public areas for a few days. No one knew if the riots would spill over into other parts of the area.

Beaches and public parks were closed and that meant no surfing for several days. It felt like an eternity.

I spent the time at my house, at school, or at Laci's house. The two of us almost got ourselves into trouble, twice, both times at my house after my mother went to work. I came to understand why young men needed to be strong; it was because young women could cause heart failure. I also came to understand that Laci was perfect in every way.

The news from the war worsened. Riots and anti-war protests began to take on similar tactics and the whole thing began to muddle.

I just wanted to get back to the waves.

Joe and Lelani were in Tahiti, the island paradise competing in the next leg of the Tour. Amazingly, Joe fell in his final ride and placed second to Taj Brown.

Lelani noticed that Joe was growing more silent as the days went by.

"Joe, what's wrong?" she asked one day after the Tahiti competition.

"Nothing's wrong," he replied, "I can't win every meet. I'm surfing with the world's greatest surfers."

Lelani put her arms around his neck.

"I know," she said, "But you've been growing quiet lately."

Joe shrugged.

"Things in the world," he replied softly, "You know, Rod, the war, the violence at home."

"The bad vibe," Lelani said, nodding sadly, "You need to let the waves take it. You go out there and you let go."

Joe continued to be quiet for a while, pondering what seemed to him to be overly-simplistic, but it was coming from a Hawaiian who never really looked at life in the hard then-and-now.

He thought about Rod, about how he came home, drained, couldn't ride, and then signed up again to return to Vietnam. It was like addiction.

Over and over he questioned why Rod or any sane person would put himself in harm's way repeatedly.

Lelani brought Joe in close and lowered his face to her chest, more of a maternal move than a sexual one.

Joe's eyes watered.

"Rod and I go way back to grade school," Joe said wistfully, "Like brothers, we went everywhere together, did everything together, even bought that old Woody together and fixed it up in auto-shop together."

Lelani remained silent but put her hand on Joe's shoulder.

"He was as good a surfer as me," Joe continued, "He could be here right now…or maybe I should be there right now."

Lelani understood about family, Hawaiians were big on it. If any member of her own family became ill or got into trouble the whole family would show up—aunts, uncles, cousins, even cousins thrice removed. She understood Joe and his pain. She also knew that each person had their own destiny, outside the family.

Lelani squeezed Joe's shoulder.

"It's hard to be close to someone and know that your destinies lay apart," she said softly.

Joe sighed.

"But in this case, Rod made a choice and I made another choice," he said, "Our destinies are somewhere on the paths we've chosen."

Lelani put her other arm around him.

"But the choices you make are part of what becomes your destiny."

Joe shook his head, unconvinced.

"You're telling me I can't make another choice and change my destiny?" he asked, feeling confused.

"No," Lelani replied, "But maybe you shouldn't. How do you feel when you ride a wave and drop down into the barrel?"

Joe stared at the water for a moment, watching the waves, rise, and break like the movement of a clock.

"Like king of the world," he answered simply.

Lelani smiled and brought him in close.

"And that is what you are," she whispered softly, "King of the surf riders."

This didn't solve Joe's crisis as he hoped it would have. His friend, his brother was putting himself on the line so that Joe and the others could surf and travel around the world. They would journey to all the exotic beaches where the hardest thing that happened was that the wind took a holiday and left the ocean flat for a time.

Joe began looking for news—how was the fighting going? How many casualties, how many dead?

He looked for names, he wanted to know about the riots at home, the protests, sit-ins and why the National Guard was shooting college students in the United States of America.

He felt the E8 slipping, harmony dropping out like a wave hitting the bowl. He felt a wipe-out coming on. And Lelani grew concerned. She hoped that the return to Oahu and Pipe Masters would help restore the balance to her world.

The trip was slow, and it didn't help Joe's brooding. Lelani wondered if Joe would even be able to surf Pipeline; it was brutal on its best day.

That fourth of April was not a good day at all, Joe thought back to the assassination of Dr. King.

This was no ordinary man, this Dr. King. Racism was a difficult thing to gauge, especially because Joe spent his whole life in California where racism was much less an issue, at least on the surface. Lelani knew very little of it as well because Hawaii, like California, was so diverse. Still, much of the country, particularly the South, needed a complete overhaul; racial prejudice was almost genetic to the people down there. But it existed elsewhere, too, and Dr. King wanted to bring the darkness of racial prejudice into the light. Still, a great deal of overt hatred had come out as well.

Threats were made to Dr. King's life every few minutes, and many southern city and county police departments were willing to entertain them all.

It was darkness in a dark time.

Racial prejudice made no sense to Joe or to me. Skin was simply skin and its color was meaningless. Baseball was perhaps the most telling institution that made the greatest statement about skin color. Before Jackie Robinson, black players were forced to play in their own leagues, even in their own major leagues. Of all the records of games between Black major league teams and white-only major league teams, Black teams won 64% of the time. The Brooklyn Dodgers took Jackie Robinson for financial reasons—he would make them winners. And he did.

Still, much of America was stiff-necked and it took the Civil Rights Act of 1964 to make it illegal for hotel managers and restaurant owners to make Jackie Robinson use the back door. Things did not completely change so Dr. Martin Luther King, Jr. took to the streets and to the capitol mall to push the point. And he did very well until someone pulled the trigger.

By the time Lelani and Joe made it to the North Shore, everyone was a little down.

However, only the ending of the world, not slated until December of 2012 according to the ancient Mayan calendar, could prevent Pipe Masters from happening.

Pipe Masters was becoming the premier event. It was held at the North Shore, aerials that were coming into vogue with the advent of the short-board just were not done. Whoever flew off the lip of a 30 foot wave roaring in at 50 or 60 miles an hour was generally not heard from again. If the sea could easily take the Titanic, it could take a fully-foolish surfer in less than a heartbeat.

Pipe Masters was about power and courage. It took skill to ride out a barrel that sometimes grew as long as some subway routes and the train inside that tunnel didn't keep its shape, it could spread all over a wave rider like a tsunami and crash onto a crowd without any warning.

Pipe Masters was about Big Wave riding, awesome and terrible physics, power of God, that sort of thing.

Lelani had never ridden waves as big as those of the North Shore, something to do with survival of the species or something like that.

This told me how important men were in the scheme of things.

She and Joe stayed at her aunt's house located up off Waimea. The Pipe Masters was fairly new, but had rapidly grown into the Super Bowl of surfing. It was said that Pipe Masters would soon be the crucial event in determining world champions. This meant Joe Connors would have to re-conquer and continue to conquer the Pipe. The creator of Pipe Masters, Fred Hennings, was pushing for television coverage for the event. He wanted to take the fledgling pro surfing circuit and put it on the world map alongside climbing Mount Everest and crossing the Gobi desert in a dune buggy.

The Pipe was huge and had always been there, but world competition made it dangerous. Wave riders took more chances and pushed the performance envelopes more than high speed jet test pilots.

Giant Slalom, or Super-G off the French Alps was nothing compared to a vicious thirty-foot wave roaring in at 60 miles an hour. Mountains didn't move much but mountains of water sank whole islands.

Maybe that was what happened to Atlantis.

Only waves like Teahuppo or Mavericks even came close. Neither was easy to get to like the Pipe was.

Joe walked the edge of something, something Lelani couldn't quite grasp. She took Joe to see her maternal grandmother, the one with the second sight. Her grandmother had always seen things in people, sometimes things the people themselves couldn't see.

Joe followed Lelani up onto the porch of the old house. Her grandmother sat in a high-back wicker chair. She was stooped, her hair thin and white. Both hands were gnarled but her eyes were clear, dark like Lelani's and piercing.

"Nana," Lelani said quietly, "This is Joe Connors, he's a wave rider."

The old woman smiled a toothless grin.

"A wave rider?" she replied, almost laughing, almost sing-song.

Joe nodded and took the old woman's hand in his.

"I'm from California," Joe said quietly, "From Malibu."

"Joe's the reigning world champion, Nana," Lelani added as she sat in another wicker chair and motioned for Joe to sit in a third.

"A King?" the old woman said with delight, "I am granddaughter to a king."

Joe smiled and nodded as he sat.

"There's trouble in the world, Nana," Lelani said.

The old woman nodded and looked straight into Joe's eyes, her gaze steady and level.

"There are always bad things in the world," the old woman replied quietly, "There always will be."

"Yes, but…" Lelani began.

"Joe here has let all the troubles in," the old woman interrupted, "And his soul is disturbed."

Joe held her gaze.

"Riding the waves is partly physical, of the body," she continued, "But most of it comes from the heart, the soul."

Lelani nodded.

"What upsets the soul upsets the body, what upsets the body upsets the ride," she said, "To be part of the wave requires the clarity of the wave."

Joe sighed.

"That's how I feel," Joe whispered, "Like things are muddied, the war, riots at home, my friend Rod. He signed up to go back to Vietnam!"

Now the old woman's sighed.

"And your friend is a surf rider," the old woman's said knowingly.

Joe nodded.

GSgt. Rod Wilson knelt on one knee as he held the radio handset to his ear.

*

"One Yankee Papa," he called, "This is Yankee Papa Two."

His squad knelt around him in a defensive perimeter, all facing outward along the primitive dirt road.

It was hot and monstrously humid, the air thick with moisture and mosquitoes. The squad had been on the move for two days, part of a large pincer movement in an operation called, "Thor's Hammer." There were a dozen squads sweeping through the highlands overlooking the Ashau Valley. Three minor engagements had left one of the men seriously wounded and an air evac took him out that morning. Rod's tracker, a montagnard from the mountains, had done well in two days catching a VC cadre and two small units of NVA regulars. The squad had run three ambushes and had inflicted significant casualties, but gained no documents, no hard intelligence.

"Roger that, One Yankee Papa," GSgt. Wilson said, "Two clicks northeast moving through the pass! Yankee Papa Two, out!"

He handed the set back to the radio operator who clipped it to his harness.

"All right, listen up; we've got gooks moving down through the pass toward us. We're going to setup on either side," Wilson said, "Two four man teams. Go!"

The men moved out immediately, leaving Wilson, Grayson, the radio operator, and Doc Hemmings, the Navy corpsman.

The three of them moved out straight up toward the pass.

Even the walls of the pass were difficult to see in the overgrowth. They moved carefully, watching for odd things in the underbrush—brush bent the wrong way, an unusual twist of the ground, anything.

Twenty minutes later, there were a series of three small explosions followed by the staccato of M-16 rifles. They were joined by the sound of AK-47's which ended almost as quickly as it began.

Suddenly, a black clad the boy of about 16 or 17 broke through the foliage. He carried an AK–47 and had a straw conical hat bouncing off the back of his head. He skidded to a halt and locked eyes with GSgt. Rod Wilson, USMC. The boy's eyes went wide with terror and then everything suddenly slowed down.

Grayson stumbled under the weight of the radio and Doc Hemmings was turned away listening to the sounds of battle and waiting for the call of "Corpsman!"

Rod squeezed off a three-round burst squarely into the boy's chest. For a fraction of a second, the boy's expression change to one of confusion, and then his expression went dead as his now-lifeless body crumbled to the ground.

Rod stood silently and stared at the body.

"Jesus, Gunney!" Doc Hemmings shouted as he spun around at the sudden shots.

But Rod continued to stare at the body, no thought in his mind.

"If that was him, he's dead," Rod whispered.

Both men stared at Rod.

ROBERT CURTIS

Chapter Nine

Joe was somewhat restored after the visit with Lelani's grandma, a wise old woman who read Joe's soul and seemed to heal it.

As the Pipe Masters began, Joe climbed back to the top, taking a monstrous wave, at least thirty feet, and riding it all the way in through the maelstrom of the white water. It was a joy to watch and the crowd went wild.

Lelani smiled.

On his second run, Joe broke over the lip and slipped down across the face. He really wanted to try and climb it so he turned and bounced the board upward. The board was too heavy and wouldn't do anything except turn back down and head for the tube that was beginning to form.

It was a monster! Elongating, it rolled out into the size of a water main back home. Joe laughed, it was a water main!

Joe dipped inside as it rolled over him. He held out his trailing hand to slice through the inside face, carving destiny and the inescapable songs of creation. Again, he knew this was his place, a surf rider living in the tube, the pipe, the Green Room, Emerald City in the Land of Oz.

Pipe Masters gave him his crown again, set him on top of the world. He felt better about himself and let the troubles of the world go, except for Rod. He kept the worries down as deep as he could. They left for Peru two days later, winging over the Pacific toward one of the holy grails of surfing—Chicama, the world's longest left-hand wave.

Peru was much like Hawaii. The people there had surfed since the beginning of civilization; in fact, Peruvians maintained that the ancient Mochica people were the world's first surfers. Who knew? The big difference was, in Peru, they surfed in big reed boats and it was tied to fishing.

Chicama was almost four miles long. To ride it one had to surf many small waves to get to it. And surfing back was problematic because the wave would never return you home. It rolled like a machine, setting you down back into the wave. But it was a good wave to compete on.

The competition was held in Punta Rocas, a place so into surfing that it was like religion. The party on the beach out-did anything in Hawaii or even in Malibu. After his recent domination at Pipe Masters, Joe surfed the Copa Barena competition like it was his own. He took Taj Brown by 14 points.

The people down there had this throne, a real throne made out of some kind of exotic hardwood. It was heavy and took eight large surfers to lift it. They crowned Joe and proclaimed him King of Peru, unofficially of course.

The party lasted four days and Taj Brown and Joe surfed with each other at night to just to see who could survive. Both did.

While there, Joe and most of the other surfers surfed Punta Hermosa, Máncora, a tiny fishing village that the surfers called, "un paradiso," El Ñuro, Huanchaco, Lobitos, and even Panic Point, which was, of course, different than Point Panic.

Panic Point was a place where the beginners stood back and watched. It was reef break with strong lefts and a great pipe. It was enough before heading on to Mexico.

On June 6, 1968, Senator Bobby Kennedy, brother of slain president John F. Kennedy, and candidate for President himself, was gunned down in a hotel in Los Angeles.

Kennedy, like his brother, and Dr. Martin Luther King, Jr. were men of hope for the country. They represented what could be. Bobby Kennedy had served as U.S. Attorney General for his brother when he was president.

After his brother had been killed in Dallas, Texas back in 1963, Bobby Kennedy swore that he would finish what his brother started. He wanted to form an America that was perpetually at peace, in other words, a utopia.

He was young and idealistic, and surfers who knew anything at all about politics loved him. The shock of the assassination coming just two months, almost to the day, after Martin Luther King's assassination, was almost too much for many American surfers. Some just packed and went home.

Joe started to slide into a slump again, and Lelani used her grandmother's words to help him work through it.

They made it to Mexico though Joe was somewhat solemn. Lelani could see it coming, the weight of the world bearing down.

Puerto Escondido was in the state of Oaxaca; a beautiful place with tremendous waves, a great deal of sun, and miles and miles of open beaches.

This would be the last leg of the tour before Joe and Lelani returned home to Pacific Palisades and Malibu beach.

*

GSgt. Rod Wilson led his men into the elephant grass. Normally, Rod should not have been out on the point but this was the way he operated. He knew the dangers better than anyone and he could spot trouble before it happened. Still, after the firefight, about thirty minutes earlier where the squad ran into the lead elements of what would turn out to be an entire regiment of NVA regulars, they were trying to get to the designated LZ where choppers would get them out. They knew they were being pursued, they could feel it; an entire regiment against a Marine squad, the stuff of boot camp where drill instructors would say that this situation was about even on both sides, Devil Dogs and all that macho crap. This was the real world and the squad was being hunted. In fact, it was worse than the Alamo because there were no stone or adobe walls, just the green that they hoped would swallow them up. Being in the elephant grass was both the best and worst situation for them, good because it could temporarily hide them, bad because it could hide the NVA indefinitely.

It seemed to Rod as if the landscape itself conspired against them, slowing them down and dicing them up. Eight men moved as quickly as they could, three others with difficulty and one being half-carried because he was only half-conscious. A mortar round landed too close and the corpsman gave him morphine to mask the agony of otherwise crippling wounds; none of the marines had time to be crippled.

It was a major dilemma and the prospects weren't good for any of them.

Radio traffic indicated that three choppers were on their way in, but the LZ was still a good two kilometers off through very serious country.

The staccato of automatic weapons behind them told them that the hunters were closing, brutally searching for them in the grass.

A small clearing up ahead led to another hill, and probably another and another until the LZ. Climbing those hills with wounded men would give the NVA all too much opportunity to take them before they could escape.

Thus, the Marines had no choice but to get on with it, it was their duty.

The men struggled up the small hill, Rod taking his turn helping the wounded man. They fell with him frequently and each time it took a little more edge off the morphine until he couldn't help but groan when they went down.

There was more elephant grass, the edges like razors, bleeding the squad the whole way. As they came down the last hill, Rod and another Marine set a couple of simple booby traps with hand grenades and fuse cord. They knew it wouldn't stop them, but hoped it would at least slow some of them down. Automatic weapons fire buzzed around them as they stepped back to inspect their handiwork. They both hit the ground in time to see two NVA soldiers burst from the grass on the other side of the hill. In the near distance, they could hear the choppers approaching. It would be close.

Rod fired off a couple of rounds and caught one of the soldiers in the chest. The other knelt and fired back, hitting the Marine with Rod directly in the face. Rod rolled the man over but it was obviously too late. He fired back at the NVA soldier but missed. He turned to look down over his shoulder as the three choppers dipped into the LZ and the squad was running as fast as they could across open ground. On the other side of the hill, more NVA broke through the grass, firing their weapons, kneeling, dropping down, and standing.

Rod had no time. He grabbed for his fellow Marine's dog tags but remembered that Marines never left their dead behind. Rod tried to pick him up but the fire began buzzing around him like angry hornets, chopping up the foliage around him like a lawn mower. He pulled the Marine down on the LZ side of the hill in the hopes of being able to stand up and lift the man. But the NVA started up the hill and he could not offer any resistance to slow them down.

He hoisted the man over his shoulder and started to run down toward the LZ. As he hit the bottom, the door gunners from the choppers began firing over his head up toward the top of the hill. Rod knew it was over.

He turned with the Marine over his shoulder and his weapon in his other hand. He fired at the NVA who had broken over the top but he couldn't get any elevation on them.

The NVA, on the other hand, had no problem. Rod felt the sting of a piece of hot lead as it tore through his calf muscle. He and the Marine's body he carried went down in a heap.

One of his men, Ruffalo, stood on the strut of one of the choppers and fired his weapon above Rod. Rod began to crawl, leaving his dead squad mate behind. But he didn't get far. Two NVA set up a mortar tube and dropped in a round. It fired out and landed between Rod and the choppers. Rod ducked his head as dirt flew everywhere and the ground came alive with flying lead charging toward him. He watched in the haze and swirling dust as the choppers lifted off leaving him alone.

The choppers had no choice, except they suddenly circled above laying a great deal of cover fire for Rod.

The NVA mortar men were killed and that threat ended, but then, a dozen more soldiers broke over the top, firing at both Rod and the helicopters. Rod saw the RPG streak off the hill and hit one of the choppers. It went down in flames and the other ones moved quickly away. He knew it was Ruffalo's chopper, his second-in-command, assistant squad leader, a father with two young daughters on his second tour of 'Nam. He couldn't understand why Ruffalo would do such a thing as come to this God-forsaken jungle twice, even though he himself had done it. He learned why at that moment when he saw Ruffalo give his life to try to save him.

The well-placed shot ended Rod's musings about fate and Ruffalo's heroism. Rod rested his head against the ground, two feet from where his squad mate's body lay, and his eyes glazed into the permanent thousand-yard stare. Wipe out.

*

Dave wasn't home when the two Marine officers showed up at his house in their standard issue green sedan with U.S. government plates. Too bad it wasn't Publisher's Clearinghouse with a check for a million dollars.

The Marines were dressed in their dress blue uniforms, each resplendent with medals and ribbons. The Marine Corps must have figured that the more "fruit salad," as they called it, that was on an officer's chest when he was on death notification duty, the more the death of a loved one was palatable. Look at these, it said, your son, brother, father, or husband could have had all these but he was stupid enough to get killed. It was as palatable as an iron flail in the teeth.

When the officers returned, Dave was at home and they expressed their condolences, *espirit 'd corps*, that sort of thing. When they entered the living room of Dave's house they knew they were in the home of a Marine, his Bronze Star and a large Marine Corps flag were proudly displayed. They understood how Dave felt even if they hadn't lost sons, they had all lost friends or men who served with them. In the Marines, family was family. They left Dave with the official notification from the Secretary of Defense. I often wondered if the Defense Department ever messed it up: "Greetings from the Secretary of Defense," for a death notice and, "The Secretary of Defense regrets to inform you..." for a Draft notice. The latter made perfect sense and the former aptly represented the callousness of the government and its cold, greedy defense industry cohorts.

At least that's what some people said about the government, especially the Department of Defense.

Dave called us and curtly told us what had happened. My mother and I were grief-stricken because Rod was like another big brother, another son to my mother. We sat quietly on the couch in the living room. The light was fading. In the growing dusk our faces were in shadow, our expressions hidden. Neither of us could really tell what the other was thinking.

"How are we going to tell Joe?" my mother asked finally, in a voice barely above a whisper. "Where is he now?"

"Mexico," I replied, "They're on the last leg of the tour for this season."

My mother nodded distractedly. I suspected she was searching her mind for the right words to tell my brother that he would never see his best friend again.

The papers the next day would read how a hot shot surfer from Los Angeles gave up a potentially lucrative career in professional surfing to join the Marines, fight for his country, and die in Vietnam. He would be lauded as a real hero.

It would be in the Section C of the paper—Local News—third page.

On the editorial page, a left wing, "love, peace, and understanding" editor would say how stupid the surfer was and that he wasn't a hero, but an idiot. The tragedy was that his death had saved Rod from being spat upon by hippies who waited for all returning service men and women at San Francisco International Airport.

A Military Funerals Liaison Officer showed up the next day at Dave's home and brought all the details of a United States Marine Corps funeral. Dave knew the details because he served as an honor guard on a number of them. There would be an honor guard, some general or field grade officer to give a speech, and a flag to drape the coffin and give to Dave as though he needed another one in his home. It all sounded grand. I vowed to have our own surfer's memorial and do it right.

The notification told all of us that Rod had died in an attack in a place called the Ashau Valley. I looked at a map and it was the smallest of dots. I wondered if I should do something on that map now that he was gone, maybe get some white out and blot it out. A great surfer, at least in mine and Joe's eyes, left the world on an insignificant dot somewhere six thousand miles from the shores of Malibu.

It was absurd.

We got hold of the tour's main number and they gave us a telephone number to the hotel in Puerto Escondido. When we called we had to leave a message for Joe to call us back.

Joe called later that evening. He told us that he was hanging on in the competition. We knew he won at Piper Masters and down in Peru, Finally, my mother couldn't put it off anymore. "Joe, honey," she said quietly, "I've got some real bad news. Rod was killed yesterday in Vietnam."

The phone line was quiet. The only sound was the static that engineers built into the system so people wouldn't hang up on one other when they paused in a conversation.

"Joe?" my mother called out softly, "Are you still there?"

"I'm still here. I'm coming home," Joe replied, his voice devoid of emotion. My mother knew she had to tell him, she knew he had to deal with it. He never would have forgiven us if we would have waited until he came home: "Hi Joe, you're still World Champion but your best friend got waxed in Vietnam, a shame, huh?"

Joe did not make his third heat and finished sixteenth. He arrived home with Lelani at LAX and we picked them up. Both Joe and Lelani appeared deflated and their faces were tear-streaked. Joe was devastated by Rod's death. Lelani's heart ached for Joe. To her, it felt as though the Vietnam War suddenly took the life of the world's greatest surfer.

It was sunny and the sky was what I liked to call "mystic blue." The hearse pulled right up to the grave site. Six brawny, dress-blue Marines solemnly pulled the flag-draped coffin out slowly and carefully then marched it to the grave. There were an amazing number of people there: local surfers who tried their best to dress for the occasion, beachcombers with wrinkled shirts and ties, hair combed with the dried salt holding it in place. Reporters were there. Dave was there with some of his relatives. Laci came to be with me.

The Military Chaplin began the service with readings from the Bible and some words about our place in the world. The Marine Colonel in attendance spoke about Duty, Honor, and Country. Rod didn't know about those things, except surfer's honor and the beaches of his country. Now, he was a statistic, a memory that would fade in most minds.

When the Colonel finished his speech, a bugler played taps. It was so moving that my eyes watered and Laci squeezed my hand more tightly. She'd been crying since she heard the news about Rod's death.

After taps, four other Marines in dress blues fired their M-14a match grade rifles which kept especially for funerals. They fired three sets each, a twelve-gun salute. Had Rod been a general, he would have gotten twenty one shots, but he was only a Gunnery Sergeant. We flinched each time a shot was fired. We were used to the roar of the surf, Mother Nature speaking out loud; but these rifles and bullets were something completely alien to us.

When the shooting stopped, two of the Marines removed the flag from the coffin and crisply and solemnly folded it into a tight triangle. They handed it to the Colonel and he leaned over Dave to hand it to him.

"On behalf of a grateful nation…" he said quietly to him.

I suppose the Marines thought that civilians automatically bought that solemn spiel. It sounded good, it sounded heroic. Had Rod been killed fighting invading NVA at Malibu, Huntington Beach, Doheny, or Mavericks, we would have bought it. THAT would have been defending freedom and our country. That would have been defending my mother and Laci. That would have been heroic. As it was, dying on a tiny dot on a map on the other side of the world for a cause none of us could really figure out, against people we never even met let alone had an argument with, was something else. Rod was a great surfer. He communed with the sea, knew her rhythms and moods. He amazed and entertained people and won the respect of all other surfers in the state.

Now, he was one of those numbers on the nightly news: US— one, THEM—1000. With the numbers that had been put up over the last couple of years, you would have thought that there couldn't be any NVA left. It made you suspicious when young men like Rod kept going over there and were killed.

I just knew that I wasn't going. I would sign up for the draft in a few months and then would go to UCLA with Laci. I'd have a student deferment.

Joe and Lelani stood near the casket with me, my mother, and Laci after everyone else began to leave. Dave saw Joe standing there and walked over to shake his hand.

Joe tried to hold it in.

"I should have been with him," he struggled to say, "I should have watched his back."

Dave smiled grimly.

"No, Joe," he said softly, "You shouldn't have been there. When it's your time, it's your time."

Tears forced their way out and then began to flow freely.

"War IS hell," Dave continued quietly, "I know, I've been there. If you have been there in the Ashau Valley, you would have died too. And then we'd be having two funerals."

"You don't know that!" Joe suddenly shouted and then pulled away from Lelani. His hands came to rest on the casket.

"I could have covered him, did whatever Marines do for each other!"

Dave placed his hand on Joe's shoulder.

"When death comes calling," Dave said, "We each face it alone. You know this. What was that young surfer's name: Mark something?"

"Phu," Joe answered, "Mark Phu."

"Right. He faced death alone just like Rod did, just like each of us will," Dave said, "You have to let it go, keep surfing, for Rod."

"You are telling me that's what he would have wanted me to do," Joe snapped, "Some heroic bullshit!"

"I am telling you that is what Rod would have wanted you to do because you've become one of the greatest surfers in the world."

Joe suddenly smacked the casket with his open hand causing all but Dave to jump.

"Why?" Joe began to cry.

Chapter 10

Joe sat on the beach at Malibu being mobbed by well-wishers and surf fans. Lelani kept the surf groupies at bay. Even I signed autographs as a bit of a surfing champion myself and the brother of the World Champion.

Hobie gave me Joe's old job at the surf shop and though I only had the one trophy, he insisted that I set it up anyway.

The fan frenzy wasn't going as well as it should have or maybe it was going as well as it could. Joe just lost his childhood friend, his best surfing buddy.

Laci looked at me as the crowd of kids around me thinned out.

"He just lost his best friend," she said with a tinge of frustration. "Don't they know that?"

I reflected for a moment while signing a kid's copy of the December 1967 issue of Surfing Magazine. It was the one with Joe on the cover.

"Surfers are notoriously optimistic people," I finally replied, "The excitement of the World Champion far exceeds the tragedy of his lost friend."

Laci thought about that for a moment and then slowly shook her head.

"I'm not getting it," she replied.

"Surfers, serious surfers search for the perfect wave," I continued, changing my tact a little, "The ride is everything – the waves, the sun, the wind and, the beauty of the beaches. How can a surfer let anything interfere with that?"

Laci looked at me and made a face.

"Because reality is there—wars are fought, people die," she snapped.

I almost laughed; this coming from a girl whose life was all about singing and little else. How I was still in that life was beyond me.

"Joe let reality in," she said, "Why did he do that if he's the ultimate surfer?"

It wasn't facetious or sarcastic, it was a legitimate question, and I thought about it. Joe was a surfer, so he did not go into the Marines with Rod and instead went on to win the World Cup and go on tour. Certainly he was sad about losing Rod but there was something more.

I glanced over at him and saw a bunch of kids begging him to go out on the water. He was doing his best to refuse them without hurting their feelings. Lelani also wanted him to get back to the waves but she understood the weight of family loss.

I decided to rescue him.

"I know he's in pain, but he needs to get back out there on the waves," I said to her. "I need to try to get him moving again."

Lelani nodded in agreement as I pushed my way through the crowd of kids.

"Come on, Bro," I said, taking his arm. "Let's you and me go out on the water, catch some waves like we always do."

The kids shouted in agreement.

"But you kids have to let me and my brother go out alone," I said to the group. My tone was serious but soft.

The kids voiced their disapproval.

"You all know Joe and I lost our best friend." We need time to heal and get back on the waves. What do you say?"

The kids looked at each other trying to decide whether they should cast secret ballots or just go with a voice vote. Heads began to nod.

Joe and I grabbed our boards and headed down toward the water together. There weren't too many riders out in the lineup, but as soon as they saw us, they gave way. The more seasoned veterans knew us, knew what had happened to Rod, and knew what was at stake. Those who didn't know us could tell something important was happening and they gave way. There was only one hold out; one surfer who objected to our cutting the line.

This dude looked like he wanted to be a hotshot wearing a "shorty" wet suit with a brand new short board.

"Hey, what are you guys doing?" he shouted, "Get back in the lineup there!"

The other surfers all looked at each other and two of them broke out to paddle over on each side of the new guy.

They spoke quietly to the guy. At first, his hands flew up into the air and he seemed agitated.

But the two surfers were patient and continued to speak to him.

"He's the World Champion," I heard one of them say, "The King of the World, dude, our world."

"And this is his beach, man, his waves," the other one added, "He chose this beach and we get to surf with him. What could be cooler than that?"

"The World Champion, dude!" the first one repeated emphatically.

The new guy gazed at us for a moment and then raised his hand motioning for the front.

"Sorry, man, my mistake," he called.

We continued paddling out toward him at the front of the lineup.

"You're Joe Connors?" The new guy asked with a newfound tone of respect.

Joe nodded and slapped the guy's outstretched hand.

"Just trying to get back in the water," Joe replied absently.

"Man, I thought someone like you would be out here every day," the new guy said with surprise.

Joe sighed heavily at looked out at the waves. "Been a little preoccupied the last two weeks," he said softly.

Preoccupied was definitely an understatement. In the last two weeks, Joe had returned from Mexico, visited Dave, buried his best friend, and did not touch a board or even go near a beach. Lelani had grown increasingly worried because Joe showed no interest in World surfing news. Even more disturbing, she found a brochure about the Marine Corps.

This was her worst nightmare, that Joe's misplaced guilt would cause him to leave what he loved, join the Marines, then go off to fight in an unjust war.

A swell began to rise behind us and the new guy kicked out.

Both Joe and I began to paddle and caught the wave. Standing together we began cutting down across the face. We were born to this life.

It was a smooth ride. As I turned to look back at Joe, I saw him simply step off his board in the middle of the ride and disappear into the wave.

I was so stunned I lost my focus and fell off my own board.

As the wave rolled over me, I could see Joe's board still gliding along the surface, a ghost board without a rider.

When I came up and looked around, Joe was nowhere to be found. I recovered both my board and his as I walked up onto the beach.

"Did you see that?" one kid said to the others, "He just stepped off his board!"

Laci walked up to me with a confused look on her face as Lelani rushed past us toward the surf. I turned to look.

Joe was still not in sight and that was unlike the King of the surfing world. A knot of panic grew in the pit of my stomach.

Our search grew more frantic with everyone joining in. The kids chased down the lifeguard truck.

Two lifeguards wasted no time; they grabbed their boards and their rescue floats and ran into the water.

By now most of the surfers who had been watching from the line started breaking away and joined in the search.

Several dived underneath the waves.

I gave the two boards to Laci and charged into the water myself, diving, searching. Out about 30 yards I dipped under the waves again and started down toward the bottom. There in about 15 to 20 feet of water both lifeguards were grabbing Joe who appeared lifeless.

It seemed utterly impossible because he had only been under five minutes at the most.

They swam quickly, towed him to the shore and ordered the kids to move back and give them room to work.

I could not believe it as both Lelani and I pushed our way through all the kids. As they lay Joe down on the sand, he immediately began to sputter and cough up water. He tried to sit up. The lifeguards pushed him onto the sand and turned him on his side.

He gagged and vomited up more seawater.

Five minutes!

He lay there with his eyes closed nodding to the lifeguards – yes, he was all right, just took a spill.

"Took a spill?" a couple of kids asked in disbelief, "He stepped off his board!"

The kids were correct, I was there, and my brother, the world champion surfer deliberately stepped off his board in the middle of his ride.

It was inexplicable, except to Lelani. I could see her eyes tearing up and it wasn't from the salt water.

She knew something bad happened, something just dropped out of the bowl of my brother's soul.

Joe finally sat up, his eyes vacant, and one-by-one the kids walked off and left us alone. They looked back over their shoulders trying to understand what had happened. I knew they couldn't; I didn't even understand.

At home, Joe was distracted and not very talkative. He spent much of his time watching television, seeking news on the war. Lelani grew more and more frustrated by Joe's growing depression and anger. Had she been a trained psychologist, she would have understood and known what to do. But she wasn't. She was just a girl from Hawaii who loved life, surfing, and my brother Joe.

My mom didn't know what to do either. She tried talking to Joe but he wouldn't open up. She tried sympathy, but it couldn't penetrate the wall of guilt Joe was building. She even tried to get him to go see her high school friend, Lexis, who became a psychologist and specialized in grief counseling.

"There's light at the end of the tunnel, honey," Mom would say. "It's perfectly normal to feel anger or emptiness after such a loss."

Joe just sat there silently, looking at nothing.

Joe began leaving for hours at a time, not telling anyone where he was going, not even Lelani.

One day, I noticed that several of Joe's surfboards were missing from the garage. I figured Joe took them with him in the Woody.

When he returned, I asked him what happened to the boards and he told me that he gave them to some gremmies down at the Huntington Beach Pier. The kids had no boards at all and he didn't need so many.

It was true that Joe had a number of surfboards, many from Hobie and many from the sponsor. I didn't worry about it until a few days later, I noticed more boards missing and then after that, even more.

I asked Lelani if she knew about the board giveaway. She didn't but didn't think anything of it until I mentioned the numbers.

"But why so many?" she asked, her confusion suddenly growing.

"He has maybe five dozen," I replied, "Giving away a dozen and a half wouldn't really hurt his stock, but he never gave them away before."

"Never?" she asked, her eyes filled with concern.

"Except one or two to me," I replied.

Lelani shook her head.

"I know he feels guilty about Rod's death, but at some point, he has to come out of it," she said wistfully.

I thought about it for a while as we both sat quietly in the living room.

"It's not Rod's death he feels guilty about," I said finally, breaking the error of contemplation, "He feels guilty about Rod."

Lelani looked at me and squinted in confusion.

"What's the difference?" she asked.

"The difference between life and death," I answered immediately, "They were inseparable…"

Lelani nodded interrupting me, "I know, he told me."

"Rod and Joe shared life," I replied quietly.

Lelani nodded, staring at the floor.

"Maybe they need to share…" I let my words trail off.

Lelani suddenly looked up at me.

"What?" She snapped, "No!"

I shrugged my shoulders.

Just then we heard the Woody coming up the driveway. We sat, frozen, waiting as the roaring engine sputtered to a halt, the car door slammed, and the front door opened.

What we saw in the doorway was a complete stranger.

My brother, Joe Connors, the World Champion surfer, was missing his long, blond, surf-and-sun locks; he was now completely bald.

Lelani gasped loudly and my eyes went wide.

Joe brought his hand up and drew it across the top of his bald head, but he didn't smile or appear embarrassed in any way. He shut the front door and walked past us to his room.

Lelani and I stared at each other in utter silence. We didn't know what to say. Something had changed in Joe and none of us had been able to reach him. He was leaving.

A few days later we all sat around in our backyard grilling hamburgers and hot dogs. But it wasn't like the old days. There was very little conversation and the air was thick with tension.

Joe's interest in the world political situation began to unnerve us. A couple of times we saw him sitting in front of the television during war news and heard him shout obscenities about the communists. He never cared before Rod's death. Surfers don't think about things like war, communism, or any kind of "ism". All we thought about was surfing and the big waves.

I took over the grill, something that normally Joe would do as the man of the house. But he had no inclination to tend the grill or be the man of the house.

It was at that moment I suddenly remembered the draft notice hidden under my mattress.

Joe had been home just over a month and all the changes in him had distracted me and caused me to forget about it. Perhaps some part of my unconscious wanted me to forget about it, wanted me to pretend it had never come in the mail. Fortunately, no police, military or otherwise, had shown up at the house to arrest him. It would be horrible if that happened. I imagined the headlines: "World Champion Surfer Arrested." Joe would be taken to jail without even knowing he had been drafted and it would have been my fault.

I ran into my bedroom and retrieved the notice. I returned to the back yard and pulled my chair closer to Joe's.

"Listen Joe," I started to say a bit nervously, "We received this in the mail while you were on tour and I completely forgot about it."

I held it out for Joe, creases and all, and he took it. He held it in both hands and stared at it. Carefully, he tore off the side of the notice and pulled it out.

He read slowly, almost imperceptibly, as if weighing the measure of each word.

"How late?" I asked quietly, realizing that I was responsible for any trouble my brother might get into.

Joe didn't respond right away.

"Over three months," he finally replied, thoughtfully.

"I'm really sorry, Joe," I said.

Lelani was talking with our mother and Laci when she turned to see what we were doing. Sensing something was wrong she walked over beside us.

"What's that?" Lelani asked as she pointed at the notice. Joe handed it to her.

Lelani took the notice her hands shaking slightly. As she read it her eyes went wide.

"Are you serious?" she cried, trying to keep her voice down, "You've been drafted?"

I reached over and pointed at the date.

"How long...?" she began and then stopped to make some mental calculations, "Three months? You're a fugitive from justice?"

It was as if the weight of the world came crashing down upon her. Joe seemed lost to surfing and then he was lost to her and headed either to the military or to prison. It was too much for her and she started to cry. Seeing her crying brought my mother and Laci over to us.

"What's wrong?" my mother asked in concern as she put her arm around Lelani.

Lelani handed the notice to her and Mom read it.

"What?" she cried, "You have a draft notice? When did you get this?"

I blushed. I could feel my face grow hot as the impact of what I had done hit me hard.

"Back at the end of March while he was on tour," I replied sheepishly.

"March?" my mother shouted, "Why didn't you give it to me?"

My mother never shouted. She encouraged us in everything we did and we tried to do the right thing. A draft notice, however, was beyond my judgment, and I hadn't known what to do about it. I should have trusted my mother.

Lelani told me and my mother she was ready to go home to the islands.

My mother was sad but she understood. I, on the other hand, still held out hope that things could be turned around.

"Listen," I said to the both of them, "I'll go down to the Draft Board and explain what happened. They've got to give him an exemption because he works outside the country."

Lelani wiped her eyes.

"You think that will work?" she asked, sniffling a bit.

"Sure," I replied, "They can't hold him responsible because he was on tour! It wouldn't be fair. And he legitimately works outside the country. And he's a world champion!"

Lelani obviously didn't regard the government of the United States as being fully trustworthy.

"I don't know…" she started.

"If we get this straightened out," I suggested hopefully. "Maybe we can get him back in the water before the new season starts."

My mother smiled and nodded, always the optimist.

We waited for Joe to return from one of his secret excursions, another excursion where many more of his surfboards disappeared.

Looking in the garage, all of us worried about the dwindling number of surfboards. It was as if parts of Joe himself were going missing.

When he finally arrived home we were all waiting for him in the living room.

He paused for a moment to take in our expectant faces.

"We want to talk to you," my mother said.

Joe nodded. "Talk away."

"I am going to go with you down to the Draft Board," I began, "I'll tell them what happened, that we received this while you were on tour and I forgot about it."

Joe stared at me.

"You legitimately work outside the country," I continued, "So they have to give you an exemption or deferment or whenever they call it."

Joe looked slowly at each of our faces, almost as if we were children or mentally deficient; the derision in his expression was very uncharacteristic of him.

"I went down to the Draft Board and took care of it," he said firmly.

The sudden relief on our faces was evident. Now all we had to do was get him back in the water before the new season.

"I enlisted in the Marine Corps," he added aloofly, as if it were a footnote. Then he walked into his room.

His words hung in the air like a poison cloud. A black hole of silence engulfed us.

ROBERT CURTIS

Chapter 11

There was a lot of crying when we took Lelani to the airport. Even I was teary-eyed. My mother hugged Lelani for a long time releasing her only when her flight number was called. Laci was confused about the whole thing. She couldn't understand why Lelani was going home, why she was leaving them. If she loved Joe she should stay and try to help him work through his pain.

She couldn't figure out why Joe joined the Marine Corps in the middle of a war. Nothing about any of this made sense to Laci. Truthfully, none of this made sense to me.

We waved our final goodbyes as Lelani walked through the gate.

My mother walked to the window and watched Lelani's plane pull away from the terminal and roll out onto the tarmac. In a matter of minutes she was gone.

We walked out of LAX and drove home. No one spoke. Lelani was gone, her dreams ruined. My mom's dreams of a daughter-in-law were dashed. Laci might turn out to fill that role someday, but it was still years away.

When we arrived home, Joe had already packed his small satchel, as he prepared to go off to San Diego and who knew what.

For the last two days, he had appeared happier than he had for the last month. But he remained impervious when it came to Lelani, surfing, my mother, or me. He had destiny written on his face. It was a destiny that terrified me.

The night Joe was to go to the bus terminal, Dave Wilson came by to pick him up. He asked if I'd like to come along. I wanted to. Dave was doing this because my mother asked him to. She knew she couldn't handle seeing his bus pull away as she had watched Lelani's airplane pull away.

My mother hugged Joe once and then went off to her bedroom to cry. Joe took a last look at her closed bedroom door before straightening his shoulders and leaving our home.

It was July 4, 1968.

When we arrived at the bus station I didn't know what to say. Dave simply shook Joe's hand, then Joe shook mine. He turned and walked toward the tough-looking, but smiling marine wearing the Smokey Bear hat, stood near the blue bus marked, "United States Marine Corps Recruit Depot, San Diego."

The gunnery sergeant directed people like a tour guide, shaking the hands of recruits and slapping them on their backs, and shaking the hands of fathers while offering white handkerchiefs to mothers. Something about that moment brought me back to the day Rod left home for boot camp. I pushed the memory away before I could follow it down a dark path.

I had no idea how many white handkerchiefs there were in his back pockets, but it had to be at least a dozen.

The bus pulled away and Dave put his hand on my shoulder.

"I tried to talk him out of it," he said, "People should do their duty, but they have to know what it is. Joe joined for all the wrong reasons and I told him that."

I looked up at Dave and nodded my head in understanding.

"He'll be back in thirteen weeks," he said reassuringly. "Maybe he'll be straightened out by then and have his mind clear."

"Maybe so," I replied, my voice tinged with hope.

School finally started and Laci and I were both freshmen at UCLA. She, of course, majored in music. I chose to major in psychology.

Neither of us had any idea what the future might bring. Laci elected to live on campus as her parents were paying for it. I, on the other hand, had to drive the seventeen miles to school in the old Woody, then I'd drive seventeen miles back home. On the days I works I'd change clothes and then drive another seventeen miles to Malibu and Hobie's.

On the days that I did not work at Hobie's, I stayed longer at school, under the pretense of studying. But I was really spending more time with Laci.

Every time I called my mother to tell her I would be late from school because I was studying, she would laugh and tell me that the only studying that was going to be done was in anatomy! I couldn't put anything over on my mother.

Joe entering the Marine Corps, in this day and age, was a bit like losing him altogether. After Rod and all of the guys at school who had died or been maimed, it was hard to imagine him ever coming home in one piece, let alone surfing again.

On the other side of the reality check, Joe only had to serve two years, and he could resume his career after he was discharged.

All of us entertained fantasies.

I tried to stay as close to Laci as I could but with our two class schedules it was difficult. We were reduced to going out on "dates."

One day, as we were sitting under a tree, she decided to tell me about the future. She told me she had plans to go back east to one of the great music schools.

I was quiet, taking in the news as if being sucked into a black hole. Why now? Why not in high school when the difference between us was more pronounced? Did she view me the way she did Joe, someone who would eventually become lost? Maybe the prospect of going back east was too much, too much uncertainty to build and maintain a lasting relationship. I didn't know what to make of it so I grew distant from her, trying to shake the feeling of sudden pointlessness.

The constant anti-war protests in school didn't help. Every military person was openly scorned and every combat soldier or marine was called, "a baby killer." It was beyond me. I couldn't understand why there was so much animosity toward our soldiers. Many of them had not chosen to serve but had been drawn in by the draft.

November of that year saw the election of Richard Nixon, an arch-conservative, who was bent on ending the war the right way, with a decisive American victory.

Joe came home from boot camp with a couple of weeks of furlough until he started something called "Advanced Combat Training." I thought being a marine made one ready for combat, but the Marines didn't see it that way. Boot camp turned you into a sword; advanced combat training made you sharp.

One day I walked into Hobie's and found Joe there. My mother had given him a ride while I was at school with the Woody.

"Hey, Little Bro," Joe said as I walked in. He was actually cheerful for the first time in six months or more.

Hobie thought the whole thing beyond belief—World Champion Surfer joining the Marine Corps during the Vietnam War. But he accepted Joe's decision out of respect for Joe.

"You want to go out on the water?" Joe asked.

I stared at him, stunned and surprised. Hobie nodded, indicating that I should do it quickly before he changed his mind.

I nodded and asked, "When?"

"How about now?" Joe replied almost sounding like the old Joe but without the big, long locks of hair swaying as he talked.

"We're slow," Hobie said, "Have at it!"

Hobie held out hope also. Like me he hoped that by getting back on the water, Joe might eventually come back to us and the surfing world.

I peeled off my tee shirt and was ready to go. We each grabbed a board and headed down to the beach. I noticed that Joe was a little leaner, more muscular, a little tighter, and even had more of a tan than he had in some time. Marine Corps training was obviously good for Joe in that respect.

We paddled out into the three and four-foot waves, consistent in their breaks, which was why Malibu was the place that it was.

We joined the lineup; a couple of guys waved and seemed a little unsure as to whether Joe was really Joe. Once everyone actually recognized him, a party atmosphere developed.

Joe took his turn, caught a wave and stood like nothing had ever happened. He was no longer World Champion because the new tour had started. The newspapers and magazines had been full of stories about Joe, Rod, and the Marine Corps. There were a couple of side stories about Trestles, the surfing area located in the waters off Camp Pendleton where the Marine Corps base located just north of San Diego. Surfers were always trying to get in there, but the Marine police would run them off.

Now all of that was history; there were no reporters or writers here now and we surfed with no pretense for several hours.

Joe was flawless, cutting across the waves, charging up and flying off the lip doing one-eighty's and three-sixty's.

For a short time on this late fall afternoon, the problems of the world disappeared in the whitewater off Malibu.

I managed to talk Laci into coming out with Joe and me, though it took some time because she needed to check her, "schedule."

I couldn't quite understand what was going on because too many things were happening at once—the war, riots, Joe, work, school, and the changes in Laci.

Again, the worries melted into the waves and Joe was impressed that Laci could surf so well.

"A natural," he said with a grin.

My mother enjoyed Joe being home, though she still had an aura of anxiety about her.

When Joe left for Vietnam, Mom called Lelani in Hawaii to tell her that Joe was going to land there if she wanted to see him.

She did.

Talking with Hobie, I told him about my confusion with everything that was happening in the world. Not only was I confused about the behavior of the world beyond my circle, I was more confused about the world within my circle. Hobie was wise and I knew he could help me clear my head.

I had just turned 18 and went down to the Draft Board to sign up. The war, brought closer to home with Rod and the other guys at school, was suddenly mine as well. Hobie reminded me that I had a student deferment and if I stayed in school, I could avoid being taken. That was the word he used, "taken." It made me feel as though I would be kidnapped, removed from all that was safe and familiar. I think that was exactly what Hobie wanted me to feel.

I was doing well enough in school so I let my worries go over the falls.

A real wipe-out.

*

Night watch. Joe crawled out of his hole and toward the front trenches. For the past seven nights in a row the NVA had tested and probed the lines. Ten or twelve or twenty guys bought it over that week. There were so many, no one could keep track of them. Every one of them had transferred in,"FNGs," Fucking New Guys. Some got it the very first week. One guy stepped off the plane only to get mortared before he could even dig his own grave. Joe didn't like night watch because you had to stay up for four hours. In those dark four hours you had to avoid getting killed by mortars, gunfire, or some NVA sapper who dropped into your trench with the intent of dispatching you to your ancestors. Then you had to try and catch a few minutes of sleep afterwards before taking mortar rounds all day. One whole squad went outside the wire last week to recon and the brass is still looking for them. No one knew what had happened to them. At least no one on Joe's side knew the answer. The firebase up on the hill was nearly over-run last week but constant air-support beat the enemy back.

Viet Nam was all carnage and no surf.

That's what Joe figured out about Vietnam. People like him and the other Marines were there as cannon fodder. Khe Sahn didn't hold the greatest strategic importance. However it was a place where the generals could say that they were fighting the still-remaining effects of the Tet Offensive that began on the Tet Holiday back in January of 1968. All of the NVA divisions that there were and all the Viet Cong that lived in the South, tried to take the country in one fell swoop. But the U.S. and allied military, if one wanted to call it that, had greater firepower. Although too many people were killed, the U.S. and their South Vietnamese allies triumphed. The problem, as it turned out, was that no one bothered to tell the NVA and their commander, the famous General Giap, that the Tet Offensive was over. His troops had been pounding the base with mortars, artillery, and the occasional mano-a-mano in the trenches and the surrounding jungle since January. They showed no sign of letting up even though American airpower pounded the NVA positions day and night. It was almost as if there was too much military hardware and ordnance lying around and it had to be used somewhere to keep it from piling up.

Joe wished they'd picked another place.

He relieved Hanson, who crawled out of the trench in the pitch black and began to feel his way back to his own grave. Most of these holes were around six feet deep with some sort of covering, mostly plywood and a whole pile of sand bags stacked on top. Ideally that covering would stop shrapnel from getting through the plywood and interrupting peaceful sleep. A direct hit was not really in the equation. If you took a direct hit, a telegram and an aluminum coffin, filled with whatever was left, went home.

Joe thought about surfing as he sat there, eyes opened as far as they could go. He listened for any sound, especially the clanking of tin cans against razor wire. That meant that NVA were coming through the lines and it was time to shoot the curl. He thought about Lelani and how she left, how she couldn't take the depression that he'd fallen into after Rod's death. He still thought he should have been there for Rod although Dave had told him no time and time again.

"When it's your time," he'd said to Joe, "It's your time."

But Joe couldn't help it. He'd spent as much of his life as he could remember growing up with Rod, at his side. They had been through everything together: surfing, the occasional fight, school, dating, though neither did that much until Lelani came along. But when Rod really needed Joe, he'd thought only of himself and surfing. Now Rod was dead, very dead, terminally dead.

Joe didn't even get a chance to defend his World Cup. Taj Brown finally got his third at Huntington Beach after nearly drowning up at Mavericks. He took a spill and somehow got his leash tangled around some rocks in the shallows. With the fury of the waves above him and the riptide beneath him, he'd nearly bought it.

But that was all behind Joe. Billabong hadn't been too thrilled with his leaving the tour, but he did have the draft notice to take the heat off the situation. They told him that he'd have to get back into it and probably win another World Cup to get their sponsorship back.

Uncle Sam and Joe's own guilt canceled the contract.

Now, here he was, no surfing because the waters off Viet Nam were completely pathetic after Australia and Waimea. He had no woman because Lelani's free and happy Hawaiian spirit could not deal with the downer, and he had no other prospects for the future. The Marine Corps was not his thing as it had been for Dave Wilson and maybe even Rod. Joe was a surfer with a weapon, a "gas-operated, semi-automatic, shoulder weapon," as he was trained to call it in a crisp, military fashion. That, his bayonet, and a couple of hand grenades were all that stood between Joe and oblivion.

He thought about our mother and me and let his thoughts drift back to the good old days when surfing and studying science were all he cared about. He wondered how history would treat the Viet Nam War. Would places like Khe Sahn be inscribed on monuments along with battles like Belleau Woods, Guadalcanal, Tarawa, Iwo Jima, Okinawa, and the Frozen Chosin Reservoir? Would a turkey shoot qualify as a great battle for the Corps? He didn't think so. What did they accomplish? No beaches were stormed, no sea walls breached, just attrition and the occasional short-timer who escaped with everything but his mind and soul intact.

Joe heard the clanking of cans, the sound of the battle about to begin. He reached down to pick up the flare pistol so he could light up the battlefield. It was always kept loaded so he al he had to do was wait and listen for more sound. When he heard it again, he raised the pistol and fired the flare. It arched into the sky, flared, and then began its slow descent on the end of a small parachute. As it did, it cast its ghostly, swinging light over the area in front of Joe's position.

Less than fifty yards out in front, the ground in and around the razor wire was alive with enemy soldiers.

Joe flipped the selector switch on his M-16 rifle to automatic and shouted: "Wire, wire, wire!"

His last thought was of going over the falls.

ROBERT CURTIS

Chapter 12

We stopped receiving mail from Joe, though we continued writing. My mother grew concerned and called the base in Oceanside. It took over a week for us to find out that Joe was alive and in the hospital in Saigon. He had not been wounded, he simply stopped and no one knew why. Finally, toward the end of his tour of duty, we received a telegram from a Marine Corps chaplain in Viet Nam who wrote to say that Joe was coming home by way of Hawaii.

I called Lelani in Oahu to tell her the news. She was still very saddened by what had happened between her and Joe but she was also determines to meet him there and see what she could salvage.

The call from Lelani two weeks later was not hopeful.

"Something's gone wrong, Patrick," she said over the telephone. My mother had her ear next to mine.

"What is it, Lelani?" my mother asked, certain that Lelani would know because women knew these things. It was one of the reasons why women were mothers; they generally had a deep intuition and wisdom about the human heart.

"I don't know, Mrs. C," she replied sadly, "It's as if I wasn't really there, or he wasn't. He couldn't tell me anything about what happened to him there."

My mother's face tightened.

"Did he say anything about coming home?" I asked, desperate to understand what my brother was going through.

There was a long silence.

"He just said he was going home, that's all," she replied finally. "He wouldn't talk about surfing or anything."

"Can you bring him home from Oahu?" my mother asked. She had grown fond of Lelani and thought that maybe the two of them could somehow bring him around.

Another long silence as Lelani weighed her options. She loved Joe, that was certain, but she was unsure about how broken he was. She wondered if he would ever recover, ever go back to surfing and find joy in life.

"I can bring him home," she sighed. "I can stay awhile."

My mother began to cry. I wondered if they were tears of joy or tears of fear. Some of them had to be happy tears, but only some of them.

I stood at the gate and watched as the airplane pulled to a stop. The stairway was moved up to the side exit of the plane and the door opened. Inside the terminal it was a sea of chaos: people waiting for loved ones, hippies dressed gaudily and dirtily, waiting to protest the returning service men and women. There were San Francisco police pushing the hippies back, airport security, and even MP's and Shore Patrol.

As the returning service people came through the gate, they were immediately met by booing and screaming. Paper signs flew and spittle flew. Several of the soldiers and Marines reacted by wading into the crowd of hippies and wailing on anything in front of them. MP's and metro police jumped in to separate them. The gauntlet of chaos sprang back into place.

I was the first to see Joe come through the gate though I could not believe it. Lelani was with him. His hat was sticking out of a pocket, his shirt was out of his trousers, and it was unbuttoned. Lelani was still trying to tuck the shirt into his trousers as they walked.

The first hippie who spit on Joe received a savage punch to the face from me. And though I was not a fighter, the kid went down in a heap. Other hippies tried to get at me and I grabbed one by the hair, shoving him to the ground.

Joe walked right past me with Lelani trying to button his shirt.

I slugged another hippie in the face and then two metro police officers separated me from that crowd. They actually saved lives that day because I was ready to kill.

"Joe!" I shouted, "Joe! Over here!"

A policeman asked me if I was related and I told him that he was my brother. The officer let me go and I arrived just in time for the Shore Patrol to grab Joe.

"Marine," one of the sailors said, "You are out of uniform!"

Joe said nothing, just stared the thousand yards.

"He had a rough trip," Lelani said hurriedly.

I grabbed Joe by an arm and tried to shove the sailors away.

"We'll take care of him!" I shouted as more rioting broke out near the gate, "We'll get him squared away. He just flew in from 'Nam! He was at Khe Sahn!"

The two Shore Patrolmen let go of Joe.

"You'd better," one the sailors replied, "Or we'll run him in for conduct."

I nodded.

"We'll take care of it right now," I said, shoving Joe towards an alcove.

The SP's turned to join the fray.

"Hell no, we won't go!" the chant began to rise from the hippies.

It was madness.

Lelani finished tucking Joe's shirt in and buttoned it.

"Jesus, Joe," I cried, "What happened to you?"

Mom made it through the crowd at that moment, angry, joyful, and shocked all at once.

Joe looked right through all of us.

"It wasn't Jesus," he replied in a monotone.

"What wasn't Jesus?" I asked, now completely confused.

Joe continued to stare.

Mom adjusted Joe's hat on his head and straightened it. Lelani worked on his tie.

"Wasn't Jesus on the wire," Joe said absently, listlessly.

Lelani handed our mother the thick manila envelope she had in her bag.

"It's a medical discharge," she said, "Honorable."

We decided to take Joe home by car rather than taking the transfer to another airline to L.A. We thought maybe the hours would allow him to feel more at ease with us, to rest and unwind along the road. When we arrived home we took him to his bedroom where, with the curtains open, nice bright sunlight bathed the room. He sat on a chair.

Lelani sat with him, while mom and I went into the kitchen and sat down at the kitchen table.

She opened the manila envelope and laid the contents out on the table. She began to look through some of the papers and I took a few of the others.

"His discharge doesn't take place for another two months," I said, surprised.

"And I have his orders here," she said, holding up a single piece of paper, "It says he's to report to the VA hospital for observation and evaluation."

I looked at her and asked, "Observation and evaluation?"

I shook my head.

"It's on Monday," she added.

I put my hand over hers as she put the paper down.

"I'll take him," I said, "Lelani and I will do it."

She nodded in agreement and continued to look through the papers.

"Here's one," she said, holding the paper up, "It says post-traumatic stress syndrome. Jeez, what's that?"

I thought about it for a moment as I looked at the paper.

"It says he went catatonic at Khe Sahn after a particularity brutal night action."

I smiled thinly.

"Night action," I said, "That's what you'd say to your friends on Friday night –'we need a little night action.' It sounds to me like battle fatigue, what they used to call being shell-shocked."

My mother took a moment to look away toward Joe's bedroom and then the tears started to flow.

"He was a world champion," she sobbed. "And they took it away, took him away."

She put her head down on the table and continued to cry.

On Monday, Lelani and I loaded Joe into the Woody and drove him to the VA hospital. It took three hours to finally get into admitting. Once there, we handed over the manila envelope and asked about the possibility of taking Joe home each night instead of making him stay in the hospital; the place had an air of a haunted sanatorium.

Orders were orders, they said.

The last image we had was of Joe being rolled away in a rickety wheelchair.

Lelani and I shared a questioning look. We wondered if this was going to turn into a horror story.

At home Lelani voiced her concerns.

"At heart, Joe is a surfer," she said, "He never belonged in any of these places, not in the Marines, not in the war. He'll never be healed in that hospital."

I thought about that for a while in silence as Lelani wiped her eyes.

"If we can get him into the water..." I mused.

Lelani nodded, "But Joe is hardly responsive. He's somewhere else."

I nodded.

"Well, we can go over to the beach and surf," I said, "Did you get to meet Hobie Alder at Makaha?"

She shook her head and smiled thinly.

"No, I didn't meet him but Joe talked a lot about him," she replied, "I'll go."

There wasn't much else to do. I had no classes that day and I didn't work. Worrying about Joe in the VA hospital wasn't going to help anything. We all cared about him but the government wasn't going to let him go.

We drove out to Hobie's and I introduced Lelani.

"She is the granddaughter of Duke, ah, the Duke," I said with the tone of grandeur.

"Duke Paoa Kahinu Mokoe Hulikohola Kahanamoku," she injected.

Hobie raised his eyebrows and smiled.

"The Duke, really?" he exclaimed.

We talked surfing, talked about Joe and the Duke. Hobie agreed that Joe was out of sync, out of phase as he called it. Lelani thought of it as 'out of balance.'

The government wasn't going to fix Joe, because the government broke Joe.

There was a connection between the surfer and the sea. The wave was alive with energy, drawing its life from the sun, the wind, and the magnetic field of the earth. It resonated over the entire planet.

This made surfers the original environmentalists and it was one of the reasons why surfers were laid back.

They were in harmony with nature. Their joys were simple and their stresses minimal.

War was a complete disruption of the harmony; it was an abomination to nature. A war simmered in injustice was worse.

It's just the way it was.

Lelani and I went down to the beach and surfed for several hours. The guys down there were falling all over themselves to be hospitable to the Hawaiian beauty.

And she schooled them. She surfed like an ancient Hawaiian queen, which, she essentially was. She loved standing on the board, arms outstretched, riding up on the lip as it broke continuously.

What balance, what grace Lelani had. It was a part of her being.

For the next four days I tried not to miss classes. I even took Lelani to class with me, which caused an uproar in my abnormal psychology class. I couldn't understand what the fuss was about. Lelani also came with me to Hobie's and her presence spiced that place up.

On that fifth day Joe called us from the hospital. He wanted Lelani to come and get him; he said that the therapy wasn't doing him any good. The groups were full of angry and bitter men who wanted nothing more than to get back at the government. Everything was a conspiracy, everyone was a conspirator, the flower children were right, and we all had to get out. So, Joe decided to get out. I felt a little optimistic when Joe called and wanted to come home.

Lelani became extremely agitated at his call, but she knew she couldn't leave him there. I tried to point out the positive perspective; Joe had called and asked for our help.

Lelani and I made up a simple plan. We would drive the Woody to the VA hospital and Lelani would go into the hospital to visit Joe. Pretending to be Joe's wife, she could visit without any questions from the hospital staff. With all the commotion constantly taking place in the hospital, we realized we had a small window in which to get him into the Woody and away from the hospital before someone discovered him missing. Lelani wondered if they would ever discover him missing, as clever as the government was.

We drove to the VA hospital and I parked but stayed in the car. Lelani went into the hospital to visit her "husband." As I waited I felt a little like a criminal busting a buddy out of prison.

About fifteen minutes later, Joe and Lelani walked out of the hospital with Joe still dressed in his hospital gown. I couldn't help but wonder why he was forced to wear a hospital gown. He was there for psychiatric therapy.

Joe seemed a little woozy and unsteady on his feet

"They gave me something," he said. I immediately noticed his speech was slurred.

We hustled into the car and quickly drove out of the parking lot, wheeling our way home as fast as we could.

By the time we got home Mom was there. As soon as we pulled up she ran from the house to embrace her eldest son. She kissed and hugged him repeatedly, touching his face and stroking his head.

Holding Joe's hand she led him into the living room.

"The problem is, this is the first place they'll come to look for him." I pointed out.

Lelani and Mom looked frightened.

"His orders were to report to the VA hospital," my mother said, "And if they find him missing, then he'll be AWOL."

"What does AWOL mean?" Lelani asked, her eyes watering, "Is it bad? Will he get in trouble?"

"It means Absent Without Official Leave," I replied. "During a war? Yeah, he could get in a bit of trouble."

"But his mental state," my mother asked, "Won't they take that into consideration?"

I thought about that for a minute. I didn't know a whole lot about the military, just what Rod and Dave used to tell us about the Marines. They seemed a little strict.

"I honestly don't know," I admitted. "This whole entire war is irrational, so how can we expect the Marines to act rationally?"

Lelani and my mother shared a glance.

"I can take him to my grandfather's," Lelani said suddenly, "Maybe he can help him and they would never look for him there."

The Duke, I thought?

"He lives in Newport Beach," she added, "He knows everything about surfing, and a whole lot about life."

Now my mother thought for a while—until the phone rang scaring us all. My mom got up to answer the phone, but it was just her sister inquiring about Joe.

"You have to do it, Lelani," she said, covering the mouthpiece so my aunt would not hear what she said. "They will come here first."

Lelani nodded and we immediately got up to pack some things for Joe to take with him. I helped Joe out of the hospital gown and into some clothes. He had to hold on to my shoulder several times to steady himself.

Lelani took a pencil and wrote an address on a piece of paper. She handed it to my mother.

"Don't show this to anyone," she said, "It's my grandfather's address. You might need it."

Mom nodded and folded the paper carefully holding it in her hand. I dug into my pocket for the Woody's car keys. I handed them to her.

She held up her hands.

"You need a car to get around, to school and work," she said, "Maybe you could drive us?"

If the circumstances weren't so desperate, it would be cool to drive to the Duke's house.

We loaded Joe into the Woody again. Lelani got in and directed me down to Newport Beach. In a little over thirty-five minutes we pulled up to a fairly nice house, modest sized, rock yard, ocean motif, much like all the other houses in the neighborhood.

That was good. Nothing about the property screamed surfing legend.

Lelani helped Joe out of the car, I grabbed his bag, and we went to the front door. Lelani rang the bell, and the god of surfing himself answered.

"Granddaughter!" the Duke said with a big smile, "I am so glad you came to see me."

Lelani hugged her grandfather and she re-introduced us.

"I remember you two from Makaha," he said, still smiling, "You are the brothers who surf like the wind. Welcome to my home."

We all entered the living room and sat down. There was a lot of surfing in that room: photographs of the Duke with famous people, including what looked like a couple of presidents, some well-known movie actors and actresses. There were trophies galore and several large Olympic medals mounted in shadow boxes on the wall.

The Duke went into the kitchen and came back with tall glasses of iced tea.

"Grandfather," Lelani began, "We are in trouble."

The Duke's smile faded as he handed each of us a glass and sat down in his easy chair. "In these days, we are all in trouble," he said sadly.

"Joe had a friend who died in Viet Nam," she continued, "Joe felt responsible and he gave up his crown and left the tour."

The Duke's eyes were filled with sympathy; he understood the power of friendship and family."

"He joined the Marines," Lelani said, "And they sent him to Viet Nam."

"I see," the white-haired old man said.

"He went to Vietnam," she continued, "And he lost his soul."

The Duke considered Lelani's words for a long moment, and then he leaned forward and patted Joe on his chest.

"No, no," the Duke said quietly, "His soul is in here. But his eyes have seen such abomination that their darkness has clouded his soul, it covers his soul."

Lelani and I both thought about what the Duke said.

"This is very important, Grandfather," she almost whispered, "Can you help him?"

Now the Duke sat silently for a while, sipping on his ice tea, looking off into the distance where Joe stared. I thought maybe he could see what Joe saw.

"I am not a doctor, or a shaman, or a medicine man," he said finally, "I cannot help him, but maybe he can help me."

Lelani and I stared at each other for a moment, wondering what the old man meant.

Stiffly, and with great effort, Duke stood up from his chair. He put his hand on Joe's shoulder and looked directly at him.

"Come, my friend," the old man said, the hint of a smile returning to the edge of his lips, "I want to show you something."

Joe looked up at the old man, and I helped him to his feet. Lelani and I led Joe behind the Duke as we walked slowly to his garage.

In the garage there were all the tools needed to make surfboards. I could see a grinding wheel, hand planers, hammers, saws, chisels, and oddly shaped stones. Along one wall there were neat stacks of wood blanks. The Duke went over to one stack and motioned for me to follow. He pointed to a large blank of wood and motioned for me to remove it.

"Put it on the saw horses there," he said motioning with his finger, "Right there."

The sucker must have been at least twelve feet long, about two feet wide, and it weighed a ton. But, I carefully manipulated it into place and lowered it onto the saw horses.

"I need to make a new surfboard," the Duke said, "This is Koa wood. This is the wood of the Hawaiian Kings."

Then he turned to me and said, "Thank you for bringing Joe to my home. We must now go to work on this surfboard."

I took the hint, the Duke and Joe had to work things out. Working on a surfboard would take several days, or even weeks, and the physical labor would probably help ease Joe's mind.

I patted my brother on the shoulder and I hugged Lelani. The Duke held his hand out to me and I took it. Though he was very old, his grip was still firm. And besides, I had just shaken the hand of the god of surfing.

Chapter 13

The next morning as I was getting ready to go to school, the telephone rang.

"Hello?" I answered, keeping my voice steady. I had a pretty good idea who the call was from.

It was the VA hospital and they were looking for Joe.

I acted very surprised, "You mean my brother is missing?" I asked, "Where could he have gone, he has no car and he's not even very responsive."

Before they could ask me any questions, I jumped on them, taking the offensive.

"How could you lose a full-grown man?" I raised my voice slightly. "He's my only brother; wait till my mother hears about this!"

The person on the other end of the line began to apologize profusely, and I smiled to myself.

"Call us back the moment you find him," I demanded and hung up.

I called my mother at work and told her what I said to the VA hospital. She thought that was clever of me.

Joe stood next to the Koa wood blank. He ran his hand across the rough surface.

"This will become an olo," the Duke began, "That is the ancient Hawaiian word for a surfboard."

Joe did not react, but continued to run his hand along the length of the wood blank.

"The spirit of the Koa wood is the spirit that lifts us on the waves," the Duke continued, "This wood is from the heart of the tree."

The Duke smiled at Joe.

"Do you feel the whisper of the waves?" he asked Joe.

Joe stopped for a moment and then smiled slowly.

"The whisper of the waves?" Lelani asked softly, smiling slightly.

The Duke shrugged.

"What if he can hear the whisper of the waves?" the Duke whispered back. "It will do him good."

He turned and led Joe back into the house.

After a rest in the living room, some more iced tea, and several dozen stories about surfing sixty years ago, the Olympics, and some of the movies the Duke appeared in, they fell silent.

"Grandfather, may we stay for a while?" Lelani asked quietly, "The Marines will be looking for Joe."

The Duke smiled.

"I would enjoy your company," he replied, "And Joe's."

I was at Hobie's when a jeep carrying two Navy shore patrolmen pulled up.

When they entered, I looked at them sternly.

"Well, did you find him?" I asked pointedly, a slight tinge of sarcasm edging my voice.

"You the brother?" one of them asked.

I looked at Hobie whose face was a mask.

"You know, I'm thinking of joining the Navy," I said flatly, "But I don't know if I'm smart enough."

The one who asked the question scowled. The other one laughed.

"No, we didn't find him," the sailor answered. "The hospital didn't lose him. He walked out."

Hobie feigned surprise and lifted his eyebrows.

"You mean there's a surfer walking around in downtown L.A. with his ass hanging out of a military – issue hospital gown?"

"Very funny," the sailor answered. "Look, he's officially AWOL and if either of you helped him, you're all going to be in trouble."

Hobie leaned over the counter and closed the distance between him and the sailor.

"You know what I think?" Hobie began, "I think you got guys to chase who haven't served their time, let alone gone to Viet Nam, or a place like Khe Sahn."

The sailor looked at the floor and then at his partner.

"Look, the guy's a Section 8," he said, "They're not going to do anything to him. We just need to do our jobs."

"Okay," I replied, "If I see him, I'll tell him that."

The sailor looked around and nodded.

"Nice place, good vibes," he said and then turned to leave.

"Yeah," the other sailor said as he flashed the Hang Ten sign.

The shore patrolmen drove away.

*

Joe and the Duke worked out in the garage Joe sawed carefully on the Koa wood blank.

Lelani walked in with a couple of glasses of iced tea.

She handed one to her grandfather.

"How is our craftsman doing?" she asked as she held the other glass with both hands.

The Duke nodded and smiled. "Not only does he surf," he replied, "But he has good hands for tools."

Lelani smiled.

Joe finished the cut and brushed off the sawdust. He stood back and inspected his work. The board was flat in the tail and round in the nose looking hardly anything like a modern surfboard.

The Duke indicated that he approved.

"Now we will shape the board's bottom," he said, "Make it better on the catch."

Joe lifted the board and moved it to a wooden frame, which held the board upright at an angle.

The Duke handed Joe a long hand plane.

"You plane from the edge toward the center, moving from the tail to the nose," he said, making the motion with his hands, "Like the bottom of a boat. Then, you turn it over and do the other side."

He walked to the front and ran his thumb and fingers across the nose.

"This must be no more than one-eighth of an inch," he said, "Too much, it will dip into the wave, too little, and it will crack."

Joe nodded.

"It feels like art," he said quietly.

Lelani smiled again at her grandfather. Her smile was touched with hope.

That night Joe slept better than he had in months; without the aid of an over the counter medicine or the hardcore narcotics given at the hospital.

I waited for Laci outside the Music building. She came out, greeted me, and gave me a mild peck on the cheek.

"Well," I said flatly, "What are you so excited about?"

She looked at me, puzzled by my comment.

"Lelani and I broke Joe out of the hospital," I said as we walked, "Just like in the movies."

She looked up at me again and shook her head.

"In the movies?" she echoed sarcastically. "We're living in the movies." She waved her hand all around.

I scowled, something wasn't quite right.

"What's the matter?" I asked quietly, "For the last year and a half it's been wonderful and now you seem aloof and I don't know why."

She steered us over to a concrete table beneath a tree. I have always thought these tables weren't constructed for comfort but designed to survive a nuclear attack or the next ice age.

"I've been so busy," she replied, "And the stress of auditions and placement and making sure I get to the right classroom has taken it out of me."

"What can I do to help?" I asked earnestly.

"What can you do to help?" she repeated. She looked away, her eyes avoiding mine.

"That's what I asked," I said.

"I just need space," she replied. I thought about that one for a minute, the one thing she had lately was space. I was so busy with my classes, work, and now with Joe, that I hadn't given her the kind of attention she deserved.

"Space?" I said, "I have been so busy with my own stuff I don't think I've given you the attention you need."

It was her turn to think long and hard.

"Let me ask you this," I injected, "Do you love me?"

For some reason, the question seemed to hit her in the face, and she almost recoiled.

It never occurred to me that she might not know what love was. Perhaps her childhood had been isolated in some way; perhaps she'd been hurt in some way I knew nothing about.

"I don't know if I know what love is," she finally replied, her voice barely audible and she continued to avoid looking at me.

I felt a lump grow in my throat and my eyes grew moist. We had been together for a year and a half. How could all that end so suddenly?

I thought for another moment.

"How do you feel when I am out on the water?" I asked.

"At first I always worried that you would get hurt," she replied, "And then when you taught me how to ride, I didn't worry so much."

"Why do you think you worried?" I asked.

She thought again.

"Because I care for you and I don't want to see you get hurt," she whispered. Her voice shook a little and I could tell this was very emotional for her too.

"Is that love?" I asked, taking her hand in mine.

She looked down at our hands and I could see her eyes moistening.

"And when you read the poetry I write for you, how does it make you feel?" I continued.

"You haven't written any in a while," she replied.

"That's not the question," I said, "How does it make you feel?"

She looked around, trying to find the right words.

"Like I am the most special person in the world," she said quietly.

"The 'most special' to whom?" I asked. Had we still been in high school, the tent would have folded right here. But Joe and Lelani taught me a thing or two about love.

"To you," she whispered.

I took my other hand and put it under her chin lifting her face. She closed her eyes and I kissed her gently, not a peck but a deepening kiss that started slowly and then caused other students to stop in amazement.

"That's right," I whispered back, "To me."

*

Joe worked hard on the board; he worked up a legitimate sweat.

The top of the board lay flat and the edges were rounded or "eased" as the Duke called it.

Joe, Lelani, and the Duke stood together to look at the roughly finished board.

"That is an olo," the Duke said. "Now we must seal the skin of the wood."

He walked to his workbench and picked up a dark object to bring to Joe. It was made of volcanic rock, it was round, flat on the bottom, and the top had a carved handhold.

"You must smooth and seal the wood with this stone," the Duke said, "This came from Mauna Loa, from the Big Island."

Joe had studied volcanoes in school and knew about them. Mauna Loa was one of the big volcanoes that formed the big island of Hawaii.

Joe took the stone from the Duke and measured the weight in his hands. It was not that heavy, but the large pores in the stone would cut the wood.

"Stroke with the stone following the grain of the wood," the Duke instructed.

Joe sat the stone against the surface of the wood and pushed down and forward. He repeated the process, and soon sawdust began to appear.

This work went on for hours, and the sawdust mixed with the poison of war as it fell to the floor.

Lelani and the Duke left him to his work.

Joe began to remember the clockwork waves of his beloved Malibu. He remembered Waimea, the colossal waves of the North Shore. Visions of Tahiti, Fiji, and Peru came to him; and then, Mexico: the call, the funeral, the horror of the war rushed back to him.

His tears began to flow freely as he increased the frequency of his strokes. The tears fell into the wood and Joe smoothed them into the grain. The tears and the labor began their healing.

When Lelani and the Duke returned to the garage, Joe sat exhausted next to the board, the sanding stone still in his hand.

Lelani ran to him and knelt down.

"Are you all right?" she asked, her voice filled with concern.

Joe nodded slowly.

"It all came back to me," he said in a voice exhausted yet stronger.

Lelani threw her slender arms around his neck.

And she cried.

The Duke, meanwhile, ran his hands all along the surface and edges of the board.

"You are now ready to finish the olo," the old man said, "Tomorrow I will show you how to make it perfect."

My mother took the call from Lelani. Lelani told her how Joe was making an ancient olo under the guidance of her grandfather. I, of course, had already told her about the project. Lelani told my mother that all the memories came flooding back and they were purged, gone.

I walked into the room just as my mother began to cry.

"What's wrong," I asked, suddenly concerned for Joe. "What's happened?"

My mother handed the phone to me.

"Hello? Lelani is that you?" I asked frantically, "What's wrong?"

I heard Lelani laugh.

"Nothing is wrong," she replied, "Everything is right. Joe has been making an ancient olo with Grandfather, and all his bad memories came back. And now, they are gone."

I was confused for a moment.

"Is Joe better?" I asked.

"Yes, he is a much better!" she replied, "And the olo is beautiful."

I had to think about this for a moment.

"Making the olo is helping Joe?" I asked in wonder.

"Yes!" she replied, laughing, "And tomorrow he will make it perfect!"

My smile came from somewhere deep, the thought of my brother, lost in the horror of war, brought back by an ancient Hawaiian art. Who needed psychotherapy and drugs?

I looked at my mother, and raised my free hand in wonder. She grabbed me around the neck and began to laugh amid her tears. These were joyous tears.

That next morning, Lelani, the Duke, and Joe stood in the garage. The Duke went to his workbench and picked up a dark stone that was very smooth and fit comfortably in the palm of the hand.

"This is a smoothing stone," the Duke began, "You caress the wood into a radiance exposing its heart. When it is smooth like glass then it will be perfect."

He handed the stone to Joe.

Joe's arms and shoulders ached, but he felt more alive than he had in months. He took this stone with a big smile.

"I'll get right to this," he said, "I'm going to make this baby shine."

Joe worked like a man possessed. He ran that smoothing stone over and over and over the wood, sealing the surface more and more with each stroke.

Again, he fell exhausted against the now shining board, this time, with a smile on his face.

The next day, a coat of lacquer went on smoothly. Work with the smoothing stone dulled the finish but pushed it closer to glass. The process was repeated seven times and the finished olo looked like a beautiful museum piece.

Lelani, the Duke, and the now-aching Joe stood before the board.

"It is the finest olo I have ever seen," the Duke announced with great pride, "And now the olo is yours, and you must ride it."

Joe looked at the old man and smiled.

"I can do that," Joe said quietly, "I can certainly do that."

And with that, Lelani, the Duke, and Joe went down to the beach with the olo.

Joe was dressed in an old pair of his Hawaiian flowered beachcombers, Lelani in a two-piece, and the Duke in his own faded pair of beachcombers. There were a only a few surfers down by the pier, kids skipping school for the waves that were there.

Joe carried the board into the water and walked slowly until he was in waist deep.

He laid the board in the water and it floated.

Slowly, he raised himself onto the board and began to paddle.

He entered the lineup with the other surfers. Most simply nodded or smiled.

One of the surfers looked more closely, and said, "Man, you look like Joe Connors."

Joe smiled as the others in the lineup looked over at him.

"Yeah, man, you do look like him," another surfer said.

"And look at the board," a third surfer said, pointing at the olo.

Joe shrugged.

"It's an ancient Hawaiian olo design," Joe replied, "Got it from an old friend."

Joe pointed toward the beach, and everyone took a look.

"Is that the Duke?" the first surfer asked.

Joe nodded.

"You ARE Joe Connors!" a surfer exclaimed.

Joe continued to nod and reached out and took the surfer's hand. He began shaking all the other surfers' hands and there was a good deal of excitement in the lineup.

"That's me," he replied with a big grin.

There was a chorus of, "Where you been, man?"

"Fighting for Uncle Sam," Joe replied.

"That's right, I read that story," a couple of the surfers said.

"Yup, not fun," Joe said as he looked over his shoulder, "Try to stay out on the waves."

"My turn, boys!" Joe said as he felt a swell rising toward them. The rest of the surfers kicked out and the one-time World Champion began paddling to catch the wave.

He did it, perfectly, and as if by instinct rose to his feet. The board was different, long and slightly awkward at first.

He took a few steps toward middle, turned the board and started down the face of the short wave. There were no aerials to be done with this olo, just ride the wave and smile in the wind.

Joe heard applause from the lineup; the surfers shouted encouragement and Lelani jumped for joy on the shore.

It was Joe's first ride in almost a year.

Joe spent the next three hours out on the waves, riding, joking with the other surfers, and watching both Lelani and the Duke ride the olo.

Every person in the lineup stopped, even the kids, when the Duke surfed. He was seventy-nine years old and surfed like he was twenty.

The god of surfing was on the waves, and for that one afternoon, surf heaven came down to Newport Beach.

And Joe was alive once again.

Back at the house, the three of them sat in the living room resting, drinking iced tea, and reveling in each other's company.

"So, you two, what are your plans?" the Duke asked.

Joe and Lelani looked at each other; they hadn't had time to think.

"I would like her hand in marriage," Joe said quietly, but with a huge grin, "And with your blessing."

Lelani's eyes went big, totally shocked. But when she regained her wits, she jumped up and grabbed Joe around the neck.

The old man laughed, "You are getting ahead of yourself, Granddaughter. I have not given my blessing yet."

Lelani stopped in mid-kiss and looked at her grandfather.

The Duke laughed again,

"But what could I deny my beautiful granddaughter?" he chuckled.

Lelani sat back solemnly, pondering future.

"What would we do?" she asked, "The Marines are still after you."

Joe nodded, "But I have a discharge coming up, and I am officially a Section 8, so what would they do?"

"They could make your discharge dishonorable," she replied quietly.

Joe nodded again because she had a point.

"We could go on tour," she suggested.

Joe thought about that for a moment.

"Or, we could go to Mexico," he said, "Teach surfing to all the gringos, open a surf shop. That has been my dream."

The old man looked at the two of them and said, "I always say you should follow your dream and find out where it takes you."

Joe and Lelani listened attentively.

"You are both excellent surfers," he said, "You have gifts you can share with the world. And I have some money, and others might help you open a surf shop."

"Hobie would help us," Lelani said to Joe.

Joe smiled, he was facing his dream and, he realized, he had his dream girl.

Joe and Lelani obtained a marriage license, and were married at Saint Mary's by the Sea, right there in Newport Beach. I was Joe's Best Man, and my mom was Lelani's Maid of Honor. The Duke gave Lelani away.

Joe promised my mother that they would visit frequently. After all, they were only going down to Rocky Point to see what they could build. The government would never be able to get at Joe. They probably didn't care anyway, because an Honorable Discharge from the Marines showed up in the mail.

We forwarded the Discharge to Joe because we were sure that he would like knowing all of that was behind him.

As a wedding present, the Duke paid for their passage on a southbound trawler headed for Rocky Point. He gave them enough money to start a little business, and Hobie pitched in with some stock that he took down to help them get a start.

My mother and I traveled down to Rocky Point to visit, bringing the sad news that the Duke had passed away, dying peacefully in his sleep. When Lelani came back for the funeral she discovered that her grandfather left her his house and all his belongings. My mother, who was a realtor, said she would help Lelani sell it, if she wanted. Mom told Lelani that she could get a great price and the money would go to Mexico for their business. Lelani agreed.

Joe and Lelani packed up all of the Duke's memorabilia and took it with them to Mexico. They would put some of the memorabilia in their shop, they would send some to Hobie, and they would give other pieces to the Southern California surfing museums that were situated up and down the coast like a perfect wave.

ROBERT CURTIS

EPILOGUE

I drove the old Woody into the parking garage at Second Street and Oliva in Huntington Beach. I kept Joe's favorite board tied on top as a kind of monument.

The Saturday spring sun hung low in the western sky, dipping toward the sea. It was bright, but not blinding.

I thought about Joe and how the waves were running wild off the beach up in Malibu. He'd be out there on his favorite board, hanging ten or crouching low on the heel, arms spread like wings as he shot the curl and thrilled onlookers like he always did.

It didn't surprise me when my mother and I received the notice of Joe's Induction onto the Surfers' Walk of Fame. I told Laci about it but didn't expect her to be there; I didn't expect much lately.

I walked to the Huntington Beach International Surf Museum across Main Street on Oliva and stepped inside. I told them that I was here for my brother who could not come because of all his work.

Lelani was having a baby and they were ecstatic. I would soon be Uncle Pat. I couldn't believe it.

One day Joe sent me his "Everything Paper." He had a note attached to it that asked if I would take it to the Physics Department at school and show it to someone. I did and the professor who read it couldn't believe it; he just kept saying, "This could be it, this could be it!" I don't know what will become of Joe's paper but I do know that a surfer wrote it.

Outside, on Main Street, there were vendors and a band was playing on a raised platform at the far end of the street. They weren't bad at all, I thought, even though they were kids just like me:

"You can't boss my Boss Barracuda around..."

I liked the catchy car tune, and as I looked around I saw some of the great ones stand around including Fred Hennings, Greg

Knox, and even Taj Brown. I headed outside. Out there, a throng of kids were dancing wildly on the street. I spotted Laci standing alone against a lamp post. She was the girl who seemed to know my thoughts and heartaches, who felt like a healing balm whenever I was around her. Today I needed that balm.

I walked toward her and our eyes locked. The smile she gave me was filled with care and sympathy.

"Hi," I said as I leaned over to talk directly into her ear.

She put her arms around me and hugged me closely.

"Hi, yourself," she replied, also directly into my ear. And we started to dance, slowly despite the band's wildfire tune.

I looked into her bright, gray eyes and blinked. There was something in her eyes, something I suddenly understood to be my future and I was only eighteen years old!

The band finished its song and the kids cheered enthusiastically.

One of the band members then leaned into the microphone and laughed maniacally, ending with the shouted word, "WIPEOUT!"

The drummer began a tremendous riff and the guitars joined in. It was one hell of a tune, striking directly at the heart of the surfing scene. I smiled for the first time in weeks.

"That's a great song," I said to Laci, leaning in again.

She nodded.

"How are you doing?" she asked as she held me tight. She knew I really wanted Joe to be there to accept this award. He deserved it.

"Better now," I replied.

The drummer broke into a solo and the kids on the street went wild again. These kids in the band were good, I thought, better than most of the garage bands I'd heard.

When the instrumental ended, the kids clapped and cheered for longer than usual. It was a really good tune.

"You know, Joe did what he thought was right when he enlisted, even if the war is wrong," Laci said as the cheering died down. "He's found his place now, with Lelani."

I nodded.

"Yeah, I know it," I replied. "Rod was his best friend and he had to do something about it. It nearly destroyed him but now he's okay."

One of the band members leaned into the microphone again.

"We've got a new song that we hope you'll like," he said, "This is the first time we're doing it in public."

The drummer began the cadence and then leaned into his mike:

"Down in Doheny where the surfers all go,

There's big, bleach, blondie named 'Surfer Joe,'

He's got a green surf board and a Woody to match,

And when he's riding the freeways, man, is he hard to catch..."

The kids began screaming. I couldn't believe my ears and Laci grinned, surprised. Then, just as suddenly the crowd erupted.

"Surfer Joe, now look at him go,

Surfer, Surfer, Surfer Joe, go, man, go,

Oh, oh, oh, oh, Surfer Joe."

My smile widened because it seemed like someone was out to immortalize Joe Connors and I was all for it. Because I believed my big brother, the greatest surfer anyone had ever seen, was immortal.

Whenever I would go out surfing I knew Joe would be out there with me. And when I was done, I would stand on the shore as the sun dipped into the ocean and I would watch; because I knew that I'd always catch a fleeting glimpse of the silhouette of a surfer, wavering in the waning light. I would always know that surfer, and I would always love him, my brother.

Surfer Joe.

ABOUT THE AUTHOR

Robert Curtis is a novelist, poet, photographer, and an associate professor at the University of Phoenix. He holds an M.F.A. in Creative Writing from Arizona State University. He lives in Chandler, Arizona with his wife, Maria, and has three children: Jessica Anne, Robert Michael, and Jennifer Delila, three grandchildren, Taylor MacKenzie, Molly Katherine, and Cooper James. He also has a daughter-in-law, Carrie, and a son-in-law, Jim, along with two canine Americans of nefarious lineage.

Made in the USA
Monee, IL
12 April 2021